"Don't Ask"

M/M Straight to Gay First Time Romance

Jerry Cole

© 2016

Disclaimer

Print Edition v1.00 (2016.03.18)
http://www.jerrycoleauthor.com

Table of Contents

Chapter One

It wasn't that Angel hated art fairs— well, actually, on some level, it absolutely was that Angel hated art fairs. He couldn't stand all the gawking. They gawked at him, they gawked at his art, and they gawked at the price tags, wearing expressions Angel wouldn't like to try and interpret. So, it wasn't as if Angel had any objections to this art show in particular, but rather to the institution in general. This particular art show wasn't too terrible as an example of the genre, and Angel had done it the previous two Aprils with Paul, the owner of the small gallery he'd been showing at since he moved back to New York to begin his career in art therapy. This fair was precisely what he liked about art: making it accessible, making it something open to everybody. Angel didn't dislike the idea of the fair at all; it was just that he hated being on display as if he, too, were pinned to the wall and tagged.

"Buck up," Travis ordered, nudging Angel in the side. Angel still hadn't gotten accustomed to this Travis— the Travis who was now part of the cast of *Summergirl* and who wore suspenders and more product in his hair than any other person Angel knew. Travis was such a method actor, it was unbelievable. Last year, when Travis had been part of the *Buccaneer Princess* cast, he'd walked about everywhere in billowing shirts and leather vests, speaking in an accent Angel was fairly sure was mostly his own invention. The best part had been the long, shaggy hair that Angel had teased him about mercilessly. Today, though, Travis' hair was neatly cut again in designer spikes, his narrow hips encased in jeans that looked practically painted on. New York, especially in the art scene, was a melting pot, but still, Travis might have been the gayest person Angel had ever met.

"And look at *that* beautiful specimen over there," Travis broke in, as if he were reading Angel's thoughts. Angel dutifully looked. Travis was pointing at a lanky dude in all-black, with a ridiculous scrap of colored fabric wound around his head like a bandana. At first, Angel thought the kid was alone, which struck him as odd, but then he turned to talk to two guys who were so obviously military, it hurt. One had flat-top blond hair and seemed to bounce slightly with every step. The other guy had his arms crossed over his chest, biceps bulging against the cut-off sleeves of his t-shirt. His hair was probably fair when long, but was now buzzed close to his skull, and he was smiling at something the blond guy was saying.

The coil of attraction that made him a little woozy hit Angel hard in the navel. He hadn't felt it in a long time, not since Alicia, and not in this way in a really long time. There wasn't anything extremely remarkable about the man; there was no doubt that he was attractive, but he was definitely no Adonis. He was, however, what Angel suddenly wanted, right in that moment, in a way that belied logic and reason. He was wearing a plaid shirt, rolled up to his elbows, khakis, and military-issue boots. He had the black silhouettes of four shields, like coats of arms, tattooed on his forearm and an uncertain smile on his lips. Travis was still drawling on, but Angel suddenly could not comprehend a word he was saying.

Angel was studying the man's profile when he suddenly turned and began scanning the room. His eyes landed on Angel, and his face actually glowed with a grin that could have been bottled and distributed for a significant sum. He nudged scarf-head, his friend, who turned and smiled in Angel's direction. Both sets of eyes were on him, and he wondered if they were smiling because they'd caught him staring, or if they were smiling through him. Angel swivelled to face Travis and stared at his prominent jaw. For a second, he was just staring at the skin as it stretched over the muscles and bones, watching Travis' face flex in an intricate dance of words that somehow never quite translated into meaning. Out of his peripheral vision, Angel saw the threesome walking toward them.

"Say something," Angel demanded.

Travis huffed, "I've been talking this whole time, you prick."

Travis looked at him properly then, immediately located the self-doubt that had started to creep across his expression, and began spinning wildly, looking for the source of Angel's insecurities. His eyes landed on the group of strangers striding towards them.

"Surely, you can't be worried about hipster-head," Travis mumbled. Angel snorted, and Travis' eyes narrowed in thought. "Oh my, is it Crew Cut?"

Angel made an obscene noise in the back of his throat, and Travis actually tittered. Angel wondered if he should've tried to hide it better, because he definitely didn't like the gleam in Travis' eye.

"I thought this day would never come," Travis exalted, looking up at the ceiling and then at Paul, who had started walking toward them.

"Paulie, Angel has a crush on a customer," Travis sing-songed.

"How many times do I have to tell you to not call me that?"

"Paulie," Travis whined, and Paul glared harder. "Sorry, couldn't hear you over the excitement buzzing in my ears. Our little Angel has a crush."

"Fucking shit, Trav," Angel mumbled.

There was no doubting it now; the threesome was making a beeline for their booth. They were pushing through the crowd diagonally against the flow of traffic, and their path would lead them directly to the gallery's display. Angel wasn't sure what to peruse by way of a distraction. It would be pretty vain to stare at his own works, but the booth was rather bare except for his stuff and a few pieces from the other artists at the gallery. He stared at the closest chef-d'oeuvre, which was a painting of ruined desserts, and it was just mind-grabbing enough to soothe his breathing and make it seem like he was actually interested.

He heard Travis' boisterous greeting, but he didn't turn. Instead, he just stared at the overturned pies on the canvas in front of him. Travis was only rambling until Angel heard the cadence of his voice change, and he knew at once that Travis had delved completely into Lothario mode— except that he wasn't seducing women, but curly-haired hipsters with questionable headgear.

Angel wasn't usually this jittery, but honestly, lately, he hadn't been able to give a fuck about much beyond himself and his son, Finn. This inexplicable, newfound spark of attraction was alien, and made him revert to feeling like a shy teenager. The last eighteen months had been an uphill trudge since Alicia's death, and being cautious and reserved hadn't been an option. Without Alicia's income to rely upon, Angel had to get out there and put himself to work: His hectic life in Chicago, in many ways an idyll for a young artist, was no longer sustainable, and he'd been forced to move back home. Getting a job at the juvenile detention center and moving closer to his family and Travis had been so incredibly important. After all the tragedy he and his little boy had been through, forcing himself to move beyond his shyness, at least for a while, had been worth it— even though all that fronting regularly left him drained and irritable.

"You're Angel Posadas, right?" A voice jolted him out of his reverie. It was the guy with the tattoos, and he was smiling amicably, enough to knock the edge off Angel's nerves.

"Yeah," he admitted.

"My mom adores you," the guy stated matter-of-factly.

"Uh..." Angel scratched self-consciously at the nape of his neck, unsure of what to say. He hadn't known what to expect from this tough-looking man, but he certainly hadn't anticipated that. "Thanks?" he ventured eventually.

Tattoos Guy seemed to note Angel's uncertainty, moving to put him at ease with an explanation. "Just, I wanted to get her something she'd really like for Mother's Day, you know? I've been gone so long, and I'm probably about to get deployed again. I just want to make it the best day I can for her. And I saw you were selling here and she loves your stuff, ever since you were featured in Art News. I thought it would be worth a shot to at least try and buy something, since this is the 'Affordable Art Show' and all." Finger quotes. Ordinarily, finger quotes put Angel's back up, but this guy's sheepish smile somehow made them endearing and dorky rather than pretentious.

"Anything in particular you were looking for?" Angel asked.

"Oh, man, anything from you will just kill her," Tattoos Guy assured him. His cheeks dimpled when he grinned, and Angel felt his heart sink just a little, because if this guy had been a forgettable asshole, it would have been so much easier. "Figuratively, I mean," the guy added, and Angel laughed.

"Yeah, sure, everything's for sale; just let me know what you like," Angel said, and the guy beamed in response.

Tattoos Guy was a soldier, not an art critic, but he examined Angel's pieces with a careful dedication that only made him more attractive to Angel's shrewd eye. He spent the most time in front of one of the smaller paintings, an abstract cool-toned canvas Angel had called "Finn." He'd painted it shortly after Alicia had died, when he'd been so worried about how Finn was coping.

"I'm almost scared to ask," Tattoo Guy said, "How much for 'Finn?' "

"How much can you afford?" Angel asked.

"No, I don't want you to do that."

"Just tell me."

The guy wrinkled his nose. The expression, like everything else about him, apparently, was distinctly charming. "Two hundred, maybe two-fifty."

Angel smiled. "Well, that's perfect, because it's two hundred."

The guy threw him a wry look. "It's not, but I appreciate the offer. Do you have anything for two hundred? Maybe a print?"

Angel shook his head. "No, buy 'Finn.' I want you to have it." Even as the words passed his lips, he knew he meant them. The entire purpose of an art show like this one was to make sure everybody got to access the kind of artwork they might ordinarily have to pass up on, but it was more than this. The way this guy had stopped, his eyes lingering on the painting, caught at Angel somewhere in the region of his chest and tugged. It was as if, without knowing anything of the backstory of Angel and Finn or anything else, he'd understood the emotions in the painting anyway.

"You don't even know me," the guy said, flabbergasted. When Angel shrugged, he persisted, "You don't even know my name."

"So, tell me your name."

"Ryan," the guy offered, after a moment's stubborn hesitation. It suited him, Angel thought. The firm set of his mouth and the soft dark eyes seemed to belong to a Ryan. "But, honestly, do you have, like a sketch or something?"

By this point, Angel was determined. "Ryan, give me the two hundred dollars and take that piece to your mom."

Another hesitation, but Ryan was wavering. "I… okay… I really appreciate it."

"You're welcome."

He took Ryan's check and wrapped up the painting for him.

"Could I take a picture with you?" Ryan asked. "My mom would love that."

"Yeah, of course."

"Pete, come here," he barked. The blond dude he'd come with— early twenties, plaid shirt— spun around in response, and Ryan inclined his head in Angel's direction. "Take a picture, please?"

Angel stood next to Ryan and felt the heat rolling off the larger man's body. Ryan put a hand in the middle of Angel's back, and he had to hold back the gasp that threatened to escape his lips.

"Thanks again."

"Yeah, no problem."

Ryan and Pete wandered off in search of their curly-haired friend, who was currently chatting— or rather, judging by Travis' stance, more likely flirting— with Travis. Angel was well enough acquainted with Travis' body language to recognize the flirtation. He could hear Travis' rowdy laughter, and the curly-haired guy's dimples were showing on the apples of his cheeks.

"Posadas, you're such a sappy shit," Travis said as he nearly skipped over to Angel. Angel rolled his eyes.

"Tattoos guy..." Travis began.

"Ryan," Angel corrected softly, which earned him a sharp look from Travis.

"Ryan," he continued obligingly, all the same, "is going out tonight with us."

"We're going out tonight?" Angel echoed curiously. Ordinarily, their nights out were arranged well in advance, especially since Alicia. This was an unexpected burst of spontaneity, and Angel had a sneaking suspicion he knew what to put it down to.

"Fuck yeah," Travis said, with a grin and a wink. Angel couldn't help but grin back.

"But Travis, I thought we were going to cuddle tonight and watch movies," he teased, just to see Travis roll his eyes elaborately.

"Angel, my dear, I can cuddle with you whenever I want, but tonight I want to fuck that curly-haired princess."

"Travis," Angel groaned, "I don't want to hear about it!"

Travis just smirked in response.

Ryan

It took Ryan and Pete the better part of an hour to get to Mike's apartment from base on public transportation, and Ryan found himself wishing he was back at Fort Bragg, where he could travel eleven miles in less than twenty minutes. This whole big city business hurt his Midwestern sensibilities. At home, bad traffic usually meant somebody's tractor had been holding up three cars for ten minutes while it turned around in Main Street.

"That took forever," Ryan whined, as they finally pulled up in the parking lot.

"Welcome to the Big Apple, my hulking friend," Pete said. Ryan snorted.

"The only good thing about being stuck in this damn city is that I can maybe meet this Posadas guy and get my mom something good for Mother's Day. But I'd be happy to go back to Fort Bragg or, better yet, to Fort Des Moines just to get away from this traffic."

"Your mom, Midwestern housewife and art aficionada," Pete said, laughing, and Ryan shook his head, more in helpless agreement than anything.

"She's obsessed with this guy's art, man. I don't know what to tell you."

"No need to explain, dude," Pete said, waving a hand dismissively. "I think it's fucking hilarious, and so Garry-like. It must run in the family."

Ryan laughed with him, because it *was* kind of funny that this woman who hadn't ever stepped foot in an upscale gallery had such an obsession with modern art. He knew for sure that she was the only one in her book club who knew who the hell Banksy was.

They met Mike outside of his apartment, and he ran at Pete like an excited five-year-old, as if they were two little kids being reunited after one had moved away. Ryan stood awkwardly to the side as the two men embraced.

"Ryannnnnnnn," Mike drawled, and pulled him into a side hug too. Ryan had always been slightly confused by their physical affection. Maybe it was a city thing, the result of their having been brought up in a culture that was worlds apart from the dusty, uptight Midwest of Ryan's childhood. They touched so much, and it still made Ryan sort of uncomfortable, because he was worried they might somehow figure him out because of it, which was ridiculous since he wasn't even remotely attracted to either one of them. It was just the way they were— he knew that— but he couldn't turn off the instinct to draw back and look around anxiously whenever two men so much as brushed hands in public, even if it was just Ryan's guilty conscience.

"To the Affordable Art Fair," Mike said, one hand upraised like a knight declaring a tournament open.

"Huzzah," Pete cheered, matching Mike's tone enthusiastically.

"Dear Lord," Ryan mumbled under his breath.

From the moment they arrived at the fair, Ryan was instantly overwhelmed. Everyone was so artsy and trendy and obviously New York that he felt like a fish out of water. All he wanted was to find Angel Posadas, get what he came for, and then get the hell out of this place that made him feel like some uneducated hick. Mike was looking around at everything, exclaiming over a photograph of bananas which he declared would look great over his bed. Pete commented dryly that it would probably just confuse any girl or guy Mike brought home. Mike argued back that it would be fine; he was a chef, so having pictures of food wouldn't be all that confusing. Pete laughed and suggested that maybe Mike wouldn't want to be outdone by a piece of fruit in the size department; Mike just giggled and said that wouldn't be a problem. Pete just laughed, but Ryan could feel the flush creeping up the back of his neck. This was typical of the behavior that made Ryan feel out of place and lost: the casual ease with which Mike could chat about his sexual exploits, real or imagined, in a public place, without shame or fear of repercussions. Mike was bisexual. Ryan knew this because Mike had told him so on perhaps their third meeting. Ryan had been stunned into awkward, clunky silence by the revelation, so now, Mike probably thought he was a massive, homophobic redneck. If only he knew.

Turning away with a sigh, Ryan scanned the area, looking for the dark-haired man whose picture he had only seen in magazines. Angel Posadas had been featured in more glossy publications than most young artists of the similar caliber, and Ryan was pretty sure he knew why. When he spotted him in the flesh a second later, his suspicions were confirmed a thousand fold. It was all Ryan could do to actually keep his lower jaw from slacking open. Posadas was, quite simply, the most beautiful person Ryan had ever seen in his entire life, and Ryan had spent a lot of time in a lot of different places. If Ryan was going to have to actually *talk* to this man he was definitely going to need back up.

He tapped Mike on the shoulder. "Got him," he said, indicating Angel, and Mike's eyes lit up. Between them, they managed to drag Pete's attention away from the knitted cacti he was inspecting, and together they trudged through the crowd and slid into Posadas' booth. It took Ryan a minute to get up the nerve to actually approach him, even though Mike had slipped effortlessly into a fully-fledged conversation with a guy Ryan could only assume must be Posadas' friend.

"Come on, man," Pete said, his voice soft at Ryan's shoulder, and Ryan shook himself, straightening his shoulders. He'd experienced worse than this. If he could stand being shot at for months in the blistering sun, he could stand ten minutes conversation with a gorgeous artist. He caught Pete's eye in thanks and made himself approach.

He needn't have worried, as it turned out. Ryan had always nursed an intrinsic suspicion of beautiful people, but everything about Angel Posadas impressed him. He was surprised by how nice Angel was, by how genuine he seemed, but especially by how generous

16

he was. Ryan knew he was getting the painting he'd chosen for a steal; he didn't miss the sharp glare the gallery owner sent Angel's way as he packed up the painting for Ryan. Ryan wondered just how much of a discount Angel gave him, and then decided he didn't want to know.

Afterwards, asking Pete to take a picture of them, Ryan put his hand on Angel's back just to see if that niggling feeling in his gut was really the arousal he thought it might be. It had to be, of course, because Ryan was constantly falling for people at the most inopportune times. Like his sister's boyfriend at Thanksgiving, the co-captain of the football team in college, and his bunkmate at West Point. He needed to have a long serious talk with his libido, because as far as Ryan could tell, it was entirely out to get him. Right now, Ryan wanted to see the tattoos that peeked out of the top of Angel's shirt, maybe trace them with his tongue. Jesus, he was so fucked it wasn't even funny. He knew he couldn't do anything about it, though, not with "Don't Ask, Don't Tell" in force, and his whole career hanging in the balance. Other people found their way around the damn rules, he knew that well enough, but Ryan didn't have the history of support, nor the conviction in himself he needed to go that route. Even Pete— he was pretty sure he could trust Pete, but still, some part of him was so terrified of losing all that he had worked for that he didn't want to risk it and come out to him. He wasn't about to step out on such a fragile limb just because of this attraction to an artist who would only paint disasters for him.

Angel's pixie-like friend skipped past six inches from Ryan's elbow, jolting him out of his morose thoughts. Mike, Ryan couldn't help but notice, had a shit-eating grin plastered across his face. Pete, half-scowling, nudged Ryan's shoulder.

"Looks like Mike wants to get some instead of hanging out with us," he observed.

"What else is new?" Ryan joked, trying to brush aside the hollow feeling in his chest that felt a little like envy. He couldn't ever imagine being as free and comfortable as Mike.

"Oy, insulting," Mike complained.

"Typical Corrigan, getting insulted about the truth," Ryan laughed, and Mike beamed at him. This was the trouble with Mike: He really was so goddamn *likeable,* Ryan couldn't really be irritated with him, not for more than a second.

"I already told Pete you guys could come. Travis is bringing his friend along, the *artist.*" Mike wiggled his fingers.

Ryan's heart rate picked up, because he already knew they'd be going. He knew it the second Pete opened his mouth and now he knew Angel would be going, too. He was going to have to ignore his dick and think with his head, which was always difficult when he was drinking. And he knew that if he copped out of drinking, Pete would get heinously concerned and not stop questioning him about it until he gave in.

He wondered if there was any possible way to duck out now.

"But tonight was supposed to be about me," Pete whined. "I was going to hang out with my two best friends, and they were going to fawn all over me."

"Pete McAndrew, diva extraordinaire."

"Fuck off, Corrigan."

"Hmm, think I won't," Mike said airily. "Actually, I think I'm going to fuck *that*—" he gestured in the direction of Angel's friend— "under my banana picture."

Ryan couldn't help the cackle that escaped his lips, but he couldn't seem to fend off the nervous ball of energy that was forming in his gut at the knowledge of what was to come. An evening with alcohol, dancing, Mike's shameless gay seduction plan, and Ryan in the middle of it, trying to resist his primal urge to get Angel Posadas into a dark corner and learn the taste of his skin.

Chapter Two

"What the fuck is this shit?" Angel asked, as he took a beer out of Travis' fridge. He needed some alcohol to calm his shaking nerves. His fingers quivered a little as he tried to find a bottle opener in Travis' miniscule kitchen.

"It's craft beer," Travis said, rolling his eyes. "Not all of us can stomach that PBR piss."

"This is basically juice," Angel protested as he popped the cap off the Pomegranate Wheat Ale.

"Shut up," Travis said, throwing a pillow in Angel's general direction with characteristically shaky aim. Angel sidestepped the missile easily and smiled.

"That the best you can do?"

Travis rolled his eyes. "I've got to leave soon to get ready for the show tonight. I got you a pretty nice seat in the balcony."

"Not the floor, not front row, not a box?" Angel brought a hand to his chest, mock affronted. "I'm fucking disappointed, Riley."

"You become such an asshat when you're nervous," Travis said, unaffected.

"I'm not nervous," Angel gritted out. He could have cursed himself for how defensive his tone was, the protest ringing in the air.

"Oh my God," Travis said, squirming around to look at Angel head-on, "you've got it really bad for that guy, haven't you?"

Angel fixed Travis with a glare and opted not to dignify the accusation with a response, hoping Travis wouldn't recognize the silence for what it really was: a desperate attempt to keep himself from launching an even more defensive-sounding protest. He took a pull on the beer instead and was surprised to find that it wasn't half bad, even if it did taste oddly like the expensive juice his mom sometimes bought for Finn from the hippy co-op store.

"How do you fuck anyone up there?" Angel asked, falling back on Travis' couch and looking up at the sleeping loft.

"Stop trying to change the subject."

"That was a serious question."

Travis followed Angel's eyes up to his sleeping quarters, where the proximity of ceiling to mattress made even sitting upright a monumental task, let alone anything else. "The serious answer is that I don't," he said. "That's why I spent the extra money on a comfortable pull-out couch."

"Do they usually pull out?" Angel teased, unable to resist.

"I'm not going to get pregnant, you prick."

Angel snorted and added, "I'm a little offended, Riley. I thought that couch was for me."

"If that's what you thought, then I don't understand why you normally end up in the loft with me," Travis pointed out, which was a low blow, frankly, for which Angel didn't have any adequate or amusing response. Travis was right, after all. Angel did like sleeping up in Travis' bed, in the warm little space between the mattress and the eaves. He liked it all the more, in some ways, when Travis was asleep

21

there too. There was nothing at all sexual about it; Angel's relationship with Travis had never been anything but platonic. It was just that, lately, stability and comfort of the sort represented by Travis' bed hadn't been too easy to come by in Angel's life. He liked curling up in that little warm space, at first with Travis on the other side of the mattress, and then later, invariably, to find Travis had gravitated toward Angel in their sleep. Travis had a tendency to throw an arm and a leg over whoever was with him, and Angel knew it was probably nothing special about him, but it made him feel needed all the same— not that he was about to share that with Travis, especially right now.

"Whatever," Angel muttered, shifting around onto his side on the couch— which was, indeed, pretty comfy. Much as Angel liked the loft, he could see himself dozing here too, if only for a little while.

"You better not fall asleep," Travis warned, as if anticipating Angel's thoughts.

"Just a little nap," Angel yawned as he pulled his knees up closer to his chest.

"Posadas," Travis whined.

"I'm tired," Angel mumbled in protest.

"You're narcoleptic, more like."

"That's a serious medical condition." Angel attempted to throw Travis a stern look, but he could already feel the softness of impending sleep tugging at his face. He didn't imagine there was much threat implicit in his expression. Still, it was the principle of the thing.

"Maybe I'm worried you have it," Travis said. "You could be passing out at the wheel, falling down on the sidewalk..."

"Oh, whatever, man." Angel wriggled around a little in search of a more comfortable position for his arms. The worst part about sleeping was always trying to figure out where your goddamn arms were supposed to go. "I don't have a condition. I just like sleep."

"Fine, I'm setting the alarm on your phone for five. You better wake up when it goes off and you better be at my show on time, or so help you God, I will kill you."

Angel made a noncommittal noise and quickly fell into a light sleep. He heard Travis leave shortly afterward, the sound of the door slamming cutting through the mist of his doze. He knew he should get up and maybe do something productive, but there really wasn't anything he could have done productively at Travis', and going anywhere else would just be a waste of time when he had the show to get to later. So Angel let himself loll back into the comfort of the couch until, at five, the alarm went off, blaring obnoxiously. Angel thought cynically that Travis must have selected that particular sound on purpose— whenever Angel had been here in the past, the sound of the alarm, though never welcome, had always been slightly less offensive. He groaned as he rolled off the couch and began patting around on the carpet for his button down shirt. His leather jacket, he located over the back of the chair; he skimmed over the pockets for his cell phone after he'd shrugged into it and adjusted it to his liking. The phone, thankfully, was there in the front pocket where Angel had left it, and he withdrew it and quickly dialed his sister's number.

"Hello?" Sara answered on the first ring.

"Hey, how's it going?"

"It's fine," Sara assured him, and then, "Don't worry."

Angel bit his lip on what he'd been about to say. "He's being good for you, I hope?"

Sara made a dismissive noise. "Angel, he's always a darling."

"That's good. Can I talk to him?"

"Of course," she responded, and he could hear her calling Finn, although the sound was muffled as if her hand were covering the mouthpiece.

There was a rattling sound, and then, "Daddy?" Finn said hesitantly into the phone. Angel brightened immediately.

"Hey, kid, how's it going?"

"Good," Finn said, sounding like he meant it. "Auntie Sara and I made cookies. They're really yummy."

"Did she let you eat them for dinner?"

"Uh..." Angel could practically see the look on Finn's little face as he considered his answer, the way his brow would be furrowed and his lower lip pushed out in concentration. "Well, she let me have one before dinner, but she made me eat all my veggies before I could have another."

24

Angel laughed. "I'm glad you're having fun."

"Are you going to come get me tomorrow?"

"Yeah, Uncle Trav says hi and that he wants to get you from school on Monday. Would that be okay?"

"I wouldn't have to go to Mrs. Hardy's?"

"No, I will call Mrs. Hardy tomorrow to let her know that Trav was going to pick you up."

Angel cringed as Finn lets out a whooping cry of excitement. "I guess that's a yes?"

"Uh-huh," Finn agreed. "I love Uncle Trav!"

Angel had a sneaking suspicion that this was because Trav took being the fun uncle to extremes, but he didn't have the heart to get in the middle of it. Let Trav stuff the kid full of candy, as long as he was willing to deal with the resulting sugar high. "Okay, kid, I've got to go to Uncle Trav's show now, but I love you, and I'll see you tomorrow afternoon. Okay?"

"Okay, Daddy, I love you, too."

"Night, Finn."

"Goodnight, Daddy!"

Angel smiled as the line disconnected. He had dropped Finn off yesterday at Sara's and he knew Finn was fine, but he still worried. He worried about everything with Finn. He was responsible for him, for the life of this other small person, and he was just so worried he was going to fuck him up somehow. He'd felt like that a little ever since Finn had been born, but now he didn't have Alicia there assuring him that he wouldn't, making sure he wouldn't. Missing Alicia was like a physical ache sometimes, even though he knew the only reason they ever really committed to getting married, and then stayed together that long, had been because of Finn. They'd been friends more than anything, but really, that made it worse. Some guys put their buddies and their girlfriends in separate categories, but Alicia had been Angel's favorite person, his best friend. He missed her vibrant laugh, her comforting smile, her conspiratorial winks over the top of Finn's head. He missed fighting with her, picking up after her, and watching her cuddle Finn. Angel sighed heavily and shook his head, as if he could shake off the intrusive thoughts. Now wasn't the time to be dwelling on the past. He forced himself to exit Travis' little studio and lock the door behind him. He could worry later. Right now, he had a show to get to.

Angel had always been in awe of Travis' acting ability, ever since he saw him in some small improv show their first year at NYU. The magnetic way he did everything onstage drew people's attention in a way that Angel couldn't put into words but had put into art before, specifically into a vibrant painting two years back that had sold for way more than even Paul was expecting. Travis might have been an idiot a lot of the time, but he was an excellent actor, dedicated and mesmerizing.

When the curtain went down for the last time, the couple next to Angel almost immediately got up and seemingly attempted to sprint out of the building as quickly as possible. Angel was nearly a prick about it, just because he could be, but in the end, he decided it wasn't worth it and let them hurry past him.

He had to wait for Travis anyway, so he moseyed on down to the gallery and set himself up against a pillar to wait.

Soon enough, Travis texted him, and moments later, he came running out to get Angel, intending to pull him backstage, as was Travis' wont on the opening night of a new show. Angel did his best to keep smiling and conceal his disorientation as he was introduced to the rest of the cast in rapid-fire succession. This was a frequent enough occurrence that he knew better than to even try and remember anybody's name. The dressing rooms were a flurry of activity, with the backstage aspect of one show feeling very much like another, from what Angel could tell. So Angel shook hands and smiled, and meanwhile Travis wiped off his make-up, pulled on his own clothes—which weren't that much different from his costume—sprayed on some cologne and deodorant, and pulled a comb through his hair a few times. Angel thought he looked pretty good and made a point of assuring him of this, but Travis, predictably, was still pulling on his bangs as they headed outside.

"Cab?" was the first thing Travis said, as they stepped outside.

"Well, I'm not gonna fly there," Angel said, which earned him a grin and a poke in the side from Travis.

Fortunately, in the theater district, it was never very difficult to hail a passing cab, and they flagged one down easily enough. It wasn't until Travis was giving the driver directions that Angel remembered

27

fully where they were going: to the club. It had been long enough since Angel had even been a frequent club-goer; the idea of going to an unknown club with the particular intention of meeting up with a load of Army guys he barely knew was even more alarming. As the cab rolled on, Angel found himself increasingly convinced that this wasn't such a good idea, but Travis seemed to have anticipated as much. When he opened his mouth to voice his protest, Travis cuffed him across the head and cut him off, leaving no room for any further argument. Travis had a way of ending conversations that Angel had never learned any defense against.

Despite Angel's misgivings, they got past security easily enough, and slid into the club. The bass was physically shaking the floor, and Angel felt nauseated by the pulse. They found the three guys near the bar, right where the beat was strongest, vibrating up through the soles of Angel's feet. Mike was wearing virtually the same outfit he had been wearing earlier, but Travis didn't seem to mind, reaching across to take a sip of the elaborate-looking drink in Mike's hand. The blond guy had a girl clinging to his side, whispering in his ear; he was pink-cheeked with alcohol buzz and nodding, although his eyes looked a little glazed. Beside them, Ryan was leaning languorously against the bar, a plaid shirt tied around his waist, one big hand wrapped casually around a beer. He was removed from the conversation, holding himself slightly apart, but he still looked entirely more relaxed than Angel felt, hovering awkwardly near the group. He wasn't sure exactly what to do; going out really wasn't his thing. It was always too loud and too crowded. He'd rather be at Travis' place having a movie marathon. Sometimes, he thought it was a miracle that he and Travis had even stayed friends, with such diverse interests, but, then again, that was probably why they needed each other— to make up for each other's shortcomings.

Unfortunately, it didn't seem as if Angel was going to be given the option to decide his own fate tonight. Within minutes, a girl had her hand gripped on his bicep and was slurring into his ear. He nodded in what he hoped was the most noncommittal way possible and tried to pull away from her, but he couldn't seem to find a place to move where she didn't go with him. She was a persistent little thing, which he begrudgingly had to give her credit for. He was getting desperate, and probably showing it, when a hand slid onto his lower back and Ryan pressed into his space.

"Babe, I got you that beer you wanted," Ryan yelled into his ear. He threw a highly convincing scathing look at the girl gyrating on Angel's hip as he pressed a glass into Angel's hand. The girl looked shamefaced and threw a pleading look at Angel, who simply shrugged and let himself sag a little where his arm had been supporting her weight. Thankfully, she took the hint, and slinked off to rejoin her friends.

Ryan's hand dropped immediately, and Angel caught himself wishing it hadn't. When Ryan turned away, the low throb of disappointment sparked into something like alarm before he saw that Ryan was only grabbing his own beer off the bar top, offering it up for cheers. Angel, relieved and embarrassed about it, tapped his glass against Ryan's and closed his eyes as he took a long pull.

"Thanks," Angel shouted.

Ryan pressed into his personal space again so that his mouth was inches from Angel's ear and whisper-shouted, "You looked about as uninterested as I would imagine I would look."

Angel had no idea what that meant. He thought— or rather, a large part of him hoped— it might mean that Ryan was interested in men. But Angel didn't usually get lucky enough that the things he coveted on a whim were given to him just like that. Hell, sometimes, he wasn't even lucky enough to be able to keep the things he really needed, like a wife and a nuclear family and a stable life. Even if Ryan *was* interested in men (unlikely, given his military background) Angel wasn't sure he could go there just now, not with Finn and everything that had happened.

But that was his rational mind talking. The rest of him was starting to feel the effects of the alcohol and the company. He smiled in response, brightening when Ryan grinned back. They fell into a slightly yelled conversation, but it was pretty hard to carry on anything substantial with the noise level in the club. Angel half-turned to say something to Travis, wanting his support and involvement, but he wasn't there and, scanning the room for him, Angel quickly located him dancing to the pounding beat with the lanky guy—

Mike. The two of them were like a couple of storks, Angel thought with a grin: all flailing limbs and circling hips trying to get closer to each other. The blond guy— Pete, Ryan had called him— was on his way out of the door with his arm around a petite, giggling brunette. "Love in this Club" started playing, and despite himself, Angel could feel his hips swaying. He wasn't sure whether it was the alcohol, the familiar song, or Ryan's presence that was bringing him out of his comfort zone, but he wasn't about to resist.

"Let's dance," Ryan shouted.

"I don't really dance," Angel protested weakly, as Ryan grabbed his arm and dragged him out onto the dance floor. "Especially not this sober," he mumbled, but the beat had wrapped itself around the base of his spine, anchoring him in place, telling him it would be wrong to move away now. Besides that, he really didn't want to anyway, which was a strange, but welcome realization.

"That's okay, just follow my lead," Ryan whispered into Angel's ear. His big hand curved around Angel's hip, purposeful, but not controlling. Ryan began swaying to the beat, keeping Angel against him. It had been years since Angel had danced like this, in some sticky club with his guy friends, unconcerned and carefree, but he found it surprisingly easy to slip back into the groove of it. He closed his eyes and leaned his head back against Ryan's broad shoulder. He didn't notice Travis and Mike moving closer until somebody's hand was inserting itself into his pocket, and Angel's eyes flew open to the sight of

Travis up against him, a blissed out grin on his face. His hand was sweat-sticky and hot when it landed on Angel's neck, forcibly tugging him close.

"Take the soldier back to my place," Travis slurred into his ear. Despite himself, Angel felt his mouth go dry and his arousal spike in his gut at the thought, however foolish, of getting laid. He swallowed, but before he could summon a response Travis was already pulling away, winking as he maneuvered out of the crowd with his hand in Mike's. Angel turned in the circle of Ryan's arm. If it hadn't been for the alcohol, he would never have had the confidence to flatten his palms against Ryan's chest, but the shift of Ryan's muscles as he gasped gave Angel confidence, and he tipped his head back, smiling. Ryan's answering smile was a little uncertain, but Angel knew he wasn't imagining the shiver that skipped down Ryan's spine when Angel brushed his mouth against his jaw, and then his earlobe.

"Come on," Angel yelled, tugging on Ryan's hand. Evidently, whatever insanity spiral he was descending into, Ryan was falling into it with him, because he let himself be pulled along without protest.

They stumbled out of the club and into a waiting taxi. In the car, Ryan's hesitance seemed to lessen— either because they were shielded now from prying eyes or because he felt more certain of himself, Angel couldn't say— but with every passing mile, Angel's heart was beating faster. He hadn't misread this, then. He felt like a teenager, the way he hadn't in years. Beside him, Ryan's hand found its way carefully to

Angel's thigh, and Angel had to shift to hide his stiffening dick. When they arrived outside Travis' apartment, Angel moved to get his wallet out of his pants, but Ryan put a hand on his arm.

"I've got it," Ryan said.

"You already bought me a beer."

"And you gave me a huge discount on a painting that my mom is going to love," Ryan grinned, and Angel was terrified to feel the exact same dopey grin pulling at his lips. *Shit.* He didn't know what this was, and he didn't know how to deal with it. Maybe it was for the best that the thinking part of his brain seemed to have shut down for the night.

As if in a dream, Angel led Ryan upstairs, occasionally glancing behind himself as if to check that the other man was still there. The door handle slipped in Angel's fingers as he fumbled it open and pushed inside. When they were both safely inside the apartment, though, and Angel caught sight of the uncertain look once again hovering on Ryan's face, it was as if a new impulse of determination took hold of Angel. It was the work of moments to take Ryan by the shoulders and push him back against the closed door; a stretch up on his tiptoes was enough to catch Ryan's mouth, pressing their lips together. Ryan was broad, his arms muscled, and even though Angel was certainly not a small man, he felt small like this, nestled against Ryan's solid warmth. It was so different from what he'd grown used to with Alicia, and yet still his body buzzed with the knowledge that he was the one in control here, even if Ryan could change that if he wanted to.

Ryan gripped at his hips, but this time it felt like a plea instead of a command. Angel smiled into the kiss and traced his fingers along the hem of Ryan's shirt. The groan this drew out of Ryan's throat swiftly turned Angel's smile into an irresistible massive smirk, full of pride and disbelief. Spurred on by the sense of success, he dropped his mouth into the hollow of Ryan's throat. He wanted, with a fierce and sudden single-mindedness, to leave marks there, leave his mark on Ryan, but Ryan seemed to sense this, one hand coming up to brace against Angel's shoulder, holding him back.

"I won't be able to explain them," Ryan whispered, almost sadly. "I'm not a very good liar."

That was disappointing, but Angel was too far invested in this now to let the twinge of rejection put him off. If anything, it only made him redouble his efforts, wanting to realize this thing under his hands before it could slip away. He tugged on Ryan's shirt, whipping it over his head in one motion. The jeans received much the same treatment a moment later as Angel unbuttoned them roughly, wrenching the zipper down and then shoving them down over Ryan's muscled thighs. Bare now, Angel could feel the heat coming off Ryan in waves, and he couldn't bite back a moan as he leaned in to mouth at Ryan's sculpted chest.

"This isn't fair," Ryan protested. "You're still dressed."

Angel chuckled, pulled his shirt over his head, and shucked his pants off. "Better?"

Ryan grinned. "I'd say so, yeah." Then his eyes flickered in the direction of Travis' sleeping loft, and the look of lazy appreciation turned into one of apprehension. "Fuck, do we have to go up there?"

"Fuck," Angel echoed. "Not if I have anything to do with it." The pull-out couch could simply serve him once again as it had done so many times in the past. He removed the cushions as fast as possible and pulled the mattress free.

Ryan laughed his approval and shoved Angel down onto the rickety little bed the couch had now been transformed into. Angel could feel the bar pressing into his back and wondered briefly how Travis could spend most of his nights like this. Then, Ryan crawled on top of him and began pressing kisses down his chest. Angel swiftly forgot about the bar.

"You're gorgeous," Ryan said, in between kisses, and Angel shivered. Words seemed to be out of reach. He groped instead for Ryan's hair, folding his hands into the thick of it and biting his lip as he watched Ryan's mouth moving hotly over his skin.

"Can I tell you something?" Ryan asked softly, pausing with his forehead pressed against Angel's hipbone. He was breathing fast, but his eyes were downcast, as if he were avoiding Angel's gaze. He looked shy, suddenly, and Angel felt his chest flood with a sort of protective fondness.

"Of course," he said, his palm curving against Ryan's cheek.

Ryan hesitated another moment, and then pushed out the words all in a rush. "I've never done this with a guy."

"Shit," Angel hissed and sat up abruptly, causing Ryan to roll over next to him. Angel moved to sit with his back against the couch and dropped his face into his hands. "*Fuck*."

"I've wanted to," Ryan said hastily, his voice cracking with earnestness, "It's not like this is some whim I've only just had tonight, honestly, man. It's just…" He hesitated. "It's hard for me. I've never really felt like risking it."

Angel bit his lip. He wasn't sure whether Ryan had meant that statement to make Angel feel special or terrified. He wasn't sure of his own reaction. "Why me?"

"I don't know," Ryan admitted. "I guess I felt like I could trust you."

"You don't even know me," Angel said exasperatedly. "Fuck, shit, damn."

"I should go," Ryan said, and backed up off the thin mattress.

"It's late; don't go," Angel said quickly. "Shit, it's just… that's a lot of fucking pressure, man."

"It's not, really. I've just been terrified of getting caught." Ryan looked embarrassed, but when he glanced up at Angel, his eyes were bright. "It wasn't really about expectation or holding out."

"Closet, huh?"

"Military."

Angel grunted in the back of his throat. He wasn't entirely sure what to do with this information. A moment ago, everything had been leading toward one obvious conclusion, and now— "I'm still really hard," he said, grinning with one side of his mouth. "Fuck, this is..."

"Can we just continue what we were doing before?" Ryan put in. "Look, forget I said anything."

"Absolutely not," Angel protested, but then Ryan's hands were on him again, his mouth hot on Angel's mouth, and Angel groaned, feeling his resolve weakening. "Or at least... well. Maybe."

Angel pushed at Ryan's shoulder and he rolled over obligingly, giving Angel free reign to swing a leg over his hips and straddle him. Below him, Ryan's face was open with expectation, and Angel leaned forward, bracketing Ryan's face with his forearms and pressing their lips together.

"I'm not going to have your first time go like this— not the whole way, anyway. But I need to take the edge off to sleep."

"I'm not a virgin," Ryan protested. "I've had sex with girls before."

There was an edge of something in his eyes, though, that was almost relief; Angel looked at him and imagined, for a moment, how it must feel to have reached Ryan's age and have denied yourself all this time, out of fear. It wasn't anything Angel was familiar with from his own life. It certainly wasn't something that could be given up without repercussions. Angel shook his head. "It's not the same." Part of Angel

37

wished he could be chivalrous enough to push Ryan out of bed entirely, leave him to think about this properly, but Ryan was so fucking gorgeous. His cock was curved and hard against his stomach, and Angel was only a man, after all. He'd made all the allowances he could stand.

Angel fumbled with the drawer on the side table and grabbed the lube out of it. He knew it was there because Finn had found it one time when he was looking for the remote control— of course. Now, though, the sight of the little tube was more than welcome, and Angel sighed with relief as he wrapped his slick hand around Ryan and then himself. Ryan whimpered low in his throat, and Angel caught his breath, let himself move, feeling the hot silk of Ryan's shaft gliding slippery alongside his own in the hot cradle of his hand. It was second nature to let himself fall into a kiss that Ryan returned with urgency.

Ryan's hips stuttered against Angel's, and Angel ground down onto him. After that, it was as if some caged animal had been released in both of them. Ryan's fingers dug into Angel's hips; Angel felt himself rocking faster despite himself, the slick tip of Ryan's cock catching on his own, making his gut tighten with heat. The inhuman growl that escaped Ryan's lips made Angel spurt and almost cum too soon. A moment later, they were bucking frantically against each other, Ryan's breath coming fast through his nose, and when Ryan seized up and came hotly over Angel's palm, Angel was powerless to do anything but follow. He kissed Ryan again after, as soon as he could catch enough breath; he kissed him slowly, not wanting it to end.

Soon enough, though, they were both breathing steadily again, and Angel knew it was time to accept the come down and move. With a groan, he lurched off in search of a washcloth to clean them both off and then crawled back onto the bed next to Ryan. His lids were already drooping heavily— sex always knocked him right out, and it had been a while— and he pushed his face into the warm solidity of Ryan's back. His hand slid down over the other man's body to the center of his chest. He didn't want to think about how sated he felt, or about how significant an event this must have been for Ryan, after all this time. His head was swimming, sex and alcohol leaving him blurry. There would be time for all of that in the morning.

"Night," Ryan mumbled.

"Goodnight."

***

Ryan woke up to his alarm screaming obnoxiously from somewhere on the floor. He scrambled off the bed and tried to find his phone as quickly as possible, but he could already hear Angel stirring awake.

"Turn it off," Angel mumbled, putting a pillow over his head.

Ryan flicked it off obediently, but he really did need to leave. He had exercises in the afternoon and would have his ass handed to him on a platter if he was even five minutes late. The military was a way of life for Ryan: He didn't pause to waste his time considering whether it was fair or not. It just was, like gravity or God.

As he was pulling his pants on, his phone trilled again, and he almost fell on his face trying to pick it up to silence it. It was a text from Pete telling him not to miss exercises— as if he needed to be told. He sent a reply message (less catty than it could have been), turned his phone to vibrate, and slid it into his back pocket. He glanced at Angel and considered whether or not he should wake him up. This— this whole situation— was new to Ryan. It wasn't predictable and straightforward, like Army life. Did you do the same stuff with a guy that you did with a girl? Did it matter? Ryan bit his lip on a sigh.

Angel looked so peaceful, his eyelashes long and soft on his cheeks. Ryan didn't want to disturb him. If there was also an element of not wanting to actually face up to what they'd done last night— well, Ryan was entitled to a bit of panic, as long as he kept it to himself. He scribbled down a quick note with his number on it and left it on Angel's hip. By the time Angel called back, if he ever did, Ryan might have actually sorted his head out about this.

The ride back to base was long, and Ryan allowed himself the luxury of reveling in the events of the previous night without getting anxious about the possible consequences. He was half-hard when he walked into the apartment complex on base. Pete was also walking back to his place, and as Ryan fell into line beside him, Pete just looked him over and started clapping.

"Congratulations on getting laid. She must have been a looker to get your attention."

Ryan snorted, unwilling to take the bait. "See you at exercises."

"You Lothario, Garry," Pete jeered.

"Bye, Pete."

Ryan strode off to hit the showers. This was the last of his alone time, and if he chose to spend it replaying his night with Angel and hoping he'd get a phone call sooner rather than later, that was nobody's business but Ryan's.

Chapter Three

Angel hated commuting more than anything else he did all day: more than paperwork, more than waking up early. It brought out a part of himself that he really didn't like— the raging, irritable part. Still, perhaps it wasn't too surprising that the caged monster should take whatever opportunity it could find to sneak out. After all, he had a lot to rage about.

His mom had suggested books on CD to keep his mind off the idiots on the road, and now Angel went to the local library every other week to pick up a new selection. Like most of Mom's ideas, it had actually worked pretty well. This time, he'd parked the car in his assigned spot behind his building, but was waiting for a chapter of his latest audiobook to finish. Leaving in the middle somehow seemed rude.

The lights were on in his place, and he knew Travis and Finn were upstairs, probably causing complete chaos in the tiny, two-bedroom apartment. Travis had probably already ordered dinner from the Thai place around the corner that he loved. Angel hoped that if Finn had homework, Travis had at least made sure he'd finished it, like Mrs. Hardy always did. Angel was perpetually slightly appalled that he had to worry about his kindergartner finishing his homework, but he guessed it was meant to strengthen his work ethic. Or some shit.

He trudged up the three flights of stairs and unlocked the two locks on the door. Immediately as the door swung open, he found himself attacked, as usual, by a whirling ball of energy. He groaned and told Finn he was getting too old for that, but Finn ignored his complaints and started chattering about his day. The kid was talking so fast that Angel could only understand a few intermittent words, but he got concerned when he caught "cunt," standing out clear and bold among the rest like a bad penny.

"Finn!" Angel shot a glance at Travis, who had busied himself with cleaning up the puppets on the living room floor. Given that Travis never cleaned up anything a day in his life, he might as well have been screaming, "I'm guilty."

"Daddy," Finn asked curiously, picking up on Angel's shift of mood, "What's a cunt?"

"It's not a very nice word," Angel said, as he threw his keys at Travis from behind Finn's back. Travis looked up, and Angel took a second to make sure Finn wasn't looking before flipping Travis the bird. He was many things, but not a hypocrite. "Uncle Trav shouldn't be saying it."

"But a lady was mean to him," Finn explained, his eyebrows knitting together.

"Yeah, but remember, we talked about how when people are mean to you, you shouldn't be mean back? Because then it makes you seem mean too, and makes them feel like they can be mean to you."

Finn wrinkled his nose. "Uncle Travis isn't mean. He was just mad, and she called him a bad word first."

"I know, Finn, but we don't use words like that just because we're mad at someone."

"Don't be mad at Uncle Trav."

"I'm not mad, just disappointed," Angel said, kissing Finn's forehead. Travis rolled his eyes and mimicked vomiting.

"I won't say it," Finn promised.

"Good. Now go play with your toys while I get ready for dinner."

He put Finn down and Finn took off to the bins in the living room where Angel tried to get him to keep all of his toys. Finn was usually happy enough to play by himself. Angel knew he'd let them know if he wanted him or Travis to play with him, but the kid probably needed a break from Travis' overwhelming presence. Angel understood Finn better than he'd ever understood anyone because Finn was basically a miniature version of himself. Alicia had always grumbled that she was kind of sad how it seemed most of her DNA was overshadowed by Angel's. From time to time, given what happened, Angel was sad about that too, but for the most part, he was grateful that Finn never seemed like a whole separate person to figure out. His whims and moods were rarely inexplicable to Angel.

"Did you order food?" Angel asked Travis.

"Of course. It should be here soon."

"Could you maybe refrain from swearing in front of my son?"

"In my defense, your offspring has supersonic hearing and that hag called me a flaming fag."

"Trav," Angel sighed. Trav eyed him defiantly for a moment before his shoulders slumped, and he shrugged in acquiescence.

"I am sorry. I guess. Only because nobody should hear their five-year-old say 'cunt,' " Travis semi-apologized, and Angel couldn't help the chuckle that escaped his lips; that was the best he was going to get. That was just Trav.

"So, how was curly?"

Travis actually got a dreamy look on his face, and Angel wanted to burst out laughing. Travis' lips mimicked words, but he wasn't speaking. Angel raised an eyebrow and Travis pointedly gave him the middle finger.

"Best sex I've ever had," Travis pronounced.

"Wow, that's quite a proclamation coming from you," Angel laughed.

"Fuck you," Travis said with a pinched expression, nudging Angel's shoulder.

"Are you going to see him again?"

"Yeah, we're eating at one of his friend's restaurants in the East Village on Wednesday."

"Travis has a boyfriend," Angel sing-songed.

"Posadas," Travis whined, which made Angel laugh more. "What about you and GI Joe, anyway?"

That pulled Angel up short. "Umm," he stuttered, "Not sure." He wasn't used to discussing this kind of stuff with Travis anymore. He wasn't used to having anything to discuss. For as long as he could remember, he'd been married, and Travis had been his freewheeling single friend with a new boyfriend every week. Even before Alicia, Angel hadn't really dated guys. Talking like this with Travis felt weird.

"How was Saturday night?" Travis pushed.

"It was good."

"Yeah, so what's with the 'not sure?' "

Angel shrugged. "He's military."

"And what does that have to do anything?"

"Don't ask, don't tell."

Travis raised an incredulous eyebrow. "Isn't that his business, not yours?" He snorted. "Fucking ridiculous that they're even allowed to keep that up anyway in twenty-fucking-ten, but it's nothing to do with you."

"Are you serious?" Angel shot him a look. "Travis, I don't think I could be that secretive."

"Wouldn't you be that secretive for Finn anyway, if you got with... someone?"

Angel wasn't sure whether or not Travis had meant to say "a guy" and then stopped himself. He wasn't even sure if it would have made a difference because Travis was right: Man or woman, he'd have done his level best to hide things from Finn, at least for a while. "Stop being logical," he scowled. Travis actually cackled, wrapping his arms around him and pressing his face into the tattoo on Angel's neck.

"Come on, Angel, you need to get out there."

"I don't."

"Call him."

"Trav, it was a nice night, but I don't think it's such a good idea."

46

"Yesterday, before you left, I didn't say anything because I knew you would get all miffed, but that was the happiest I've seen you since Finn was born," Travis said into Angel's skin.

"Travis," Angel reprimanded quietly.

"You should try, for yourself."

After a long moment, Angel conceded, "I'll call him tonight."

"I always win."

"Only because you wear everyone down, Travis. I wish that curly-haired fuck a lot of luck with you."

"Cunt," Travis hissed.

After dinner, Travis left and Angel got started on Finn's bedtime routine. Finn whined a little bit and Angel wondered why, out of all things, Finn didn't get his love for sleeping. Finn would stay up all night if Angel would let him. Angel started a bath and Finn collected so many toys to bring in with him that he could barely move in the tub; at this rate, Angel was going to have to add more water just to make sure that Finn got clean. Still, anything to keep him quiet.

While Finn splashed around in the bubbles, Angel sat on the toilet seat and sketched Ryan from memory. If Travis knew he was doing this, he'd never live it down. He had definitely considered not calling Ryan— had leaned strongly toward that option, in fact, out of uncertainty and a little fear— but he knew Travis would just find out and somehow hatch a diabolical plot to get them together again. Angel had, by this time, learned to avoid Travis' scheming at all costs, which meant just doing what Travis wanted him to do, or at least doing enough to appease him into not embarking on something sinister.

Angel limited Finn to two books for his bedtime stories, and he read Finn a couple of long-time favorites, books Angel remembered from his own childhood. Angel decided to ignore the fact that Finn had brought three more books into bed with him and would probably be reading them until he fell asleep.

"All right, kid, it's time to go to sleep," Angel said sternly.

"Okay."

"I love you." Angel kissed Finn on the forehead.

"Love you too, Daddy," Finn said.

"I'm going to come check on you again when the clock says eight-fifteen after I do the dishes," Angel warned.

"Mmmkay."

"You need to go to bed, Finn."

"I am in bed, Dad," Finn responded, and Angel was always slightly impressed despite himself when Finn had such smart-ass retorts.

"You spend too much time with Uncle Trav," Angel sighed and Finn giggled.

"Night, Dad."

"Night, kid."

There weren't a huge amount of dishes, but Angel used the time to make Finn and himself lunches for the next day. He picked up a few loose toys and then went to check on Finn again. Finn had a book laid out on his lap, but Angel was pretty sure he'd fallen asleep, which was really no wonder, what with

48

everything he probably did with Travis. He kissed Finn on the forehead and, indeed, there was no response. Relieved, Angel put the books back up on the little bookshelf next to Finn's bed and tiptoed out of the bedroom.

When he went back into the living room, he could feel the sense of urgency creeping up the back of his neck in waves, and sighed. He was never going to get rid of it now until he'd dealt with it; damn Travis for bringing it up. After a minute's wavering, he decided he might as well get it over with, and he dialed the number from the receipt that was left next to his head Sunday morning. It rang and rang and Angel kind of hoped for the voicemail, or even for some beautiful anxiety-clearing eventuality where the voicemail wasn't even hooked up.

"Hello?"

"Hi, Ryan. It's Angel from Saturday… err, Sunday."

"I know who Angel is," Ryan responded with a soft laugh.

"So, I'm going to skip the chitchat and ask: Do you want to go out some time?"

"Yeah, I'd like that."

Good, Angel thought, and then doubted himself. But, no, his gut feeling was definitely pleased. "Good, me too. Do you know the Yemen Café?"

"Yeah, Pete loves it." Ryan's voice was deeper than Angel remembered, warm and friendly enough to set even Angel at ease.

"I was thinking something this weekend would be great."

"Yeah," Ryan agreed easily, "Sunday's probably the best."

"Awesome."

"See you there."

"Yeah, bye."

Angel wondered if the awkwardness of that phone conversation was going to bleed into their date; he sure as hell hoped not. With a sigh, wondering if he'd done the right thing, he called Rosa and bribed her with dinner, breakfast, and fifty bucks to come over on Sunday night to watch Finn. She probably would've done it for free, but he felt guilty using his sister's generosity against her— especially when he could pay a babysitter, but he just didn't want to leave his son alone with someone who wasn't close to them more than he had to.

For the rest of the week, Angel's nerves were shot anytime he so much as thought about Ryan and their date. He was so behind on paperwork that it might as well have been a joke. He was uncharacteristically lackadaisical, and the juveniles he worked with were starting to question how he was feeling, which was usually Angel's remit, not theirs. He tried to take his mind off this unknown feeling, but he couldn't really manage it on his own. Therapy, it seemed, still hadn't gotten him enough practice.

Travis helped him, though, with his constant chatter about Mike Corrigan. Mike Corrigan was a sous-chef at one of the best restaurants in Chelsea...

Mike Corrigan defied typical gender roles... Mike Corrigan liked to watch soccer... Mike Corrigan had a banana picture above his bed that didn't outdo him. Angel couldn't remember the last time Travis had been this obsessed with someone. The last long relationship, Travis had ended right after Finn was born, and Travis' boyfriend said he wanted nothing to do with kids. As young as Travis was, he knew he wanted kids and especially wanted to be in his best friend's kid's life. Angel wondered if the hipster-head could be who Travis needed him to be.

"You need to stop stressing," Travis demanded over the phone.

"I'm not stressing," Angel mumbled as he cut up vegetables for dinner.

"You totally are."

"Shuddup."

"It's cute."

"Travis, I have to feed my son and be a responsible adult now."

"Bye, Angelie Boo."

"You're insufferable."

"You love it."

"Bye, Trav."

On Sunday, his sister showed up in yoga pants and a hand-me-down NYU sweatshirt with her hair in a bun and a messenger bag slung over her shoulder. She had the Finn Survival Pack with her: coloring books, a pack of crayons, and a grow-your-own-dinosaur pack in her hand. She smiled winningly at Angel and he threw her a scowl in return, letting it melt into laughter when she commenced beating him over the head with the messenger bag. Still, it was only partly a joke. The last thing Finn needed was overstimulation.

"Do you buy him that stuff just to piss me off?" Angel asked.

"Angel, honey, he needs to experience art like every other child his age," Rosa informed him, pressing her bag into his chest.

"Rosa," Angel sighed.

"Brother dearest, this is how life works when you ask me to traipse over to Queens from Columbia. It took me over an hour."

"I'm sorry."

"Psh, all in a day's work to see my favorite brother."

"Finn, come say hi to your aunt," Angel called.

"Auntie Rosa," Finn screamed, as he careened into the foyer. He plowed into her, wrapping his arms around her waist, and she squeaked for his benefit as she cuddled him back.

"Finnaroni, are we going to have macaroni for dinner?"

"You're silly."

"I know. It's part of my charm."

"Are you going to be okay with Aunt Rosa?" Angel asked Finn, delicately brushing the hair off his forehead while Rosa rolled her eyes.

"Yeah, Dad," Finn declared with slightly worrying enthusiasm as he shook out some kind of dance.

"Thanks again, Rosa."

"Get it in, brotha."

"You're embarrassing."

"Also part of my charm," Rosa called as Finn dragged her to the kitchen.

The drive wasn't that long, so Angel didn't play the book tapes. Instead, he listened to the rhythmic crooning of Aman Jones, one of his mom's favorites. Angel had been listening to Aman Jones since he was eleven, and he still got the same blessed serene feeling whenever the music played. Right now, it felt like he needed that feeling.

He arrived a few minutes late and figured that, if this was going to last between him and Ryan, that Ryan might as well figure out now rather than later that "late" was Angel's default setting. Of course, Ryan wasn't late. He was probably there fifteen minutes early, which was just Angel's luck. He walked swiftly to the table where Ryan was sitting, wearing another plaid shirt and jeans.

"Sorry I'm late," Angel said, sliding off his jacket.

"No worries," Ryan responded, looking up and grinning brightly at him, while Angel fiddled with the sleeves of his sweater. Angel found his good-naturedness to be both endearing and overwhelming. Angel knew he could never be as nice and sweet and open as this guy in front of him. It was something that he'd always known: He wasn't nearly as nice of a person as he could be or should be.

Angel sat down and picked up the menu just to have something to do, even though he knew already he was going to order Saltah and a special Yemen tea. He read the descriptions as he would at a restaurant he'd never been to before, but this was another one of Travis' favorite restaurants, and Angel could probably describe every item on the menu.

"I was thinking about getting the Chicken Supreme," Ryan said. "I'm not a very adventurous… food… eater." Ryan scrunched up his nose, as if knowing there had to be a better term than "food eater," but unable to put a finger on it.

"That's what Finn usually gets," Angel said off-handedly, and then immediately wanted to beat himself over the head with the menu and then maybe the plate, and then maybe the chair he was sitting on. It felt sturdy enough to knock him out. He liked Ryan, and now, he was probably going to scare him away because Ryan looked perturbed, as if Angel had brought up a boyfriend or an ex. The problem was that it was worse than that. He'd brought up a son. Ryan didn't ask verbally, but his eyes said it all. So Angel just leaped right in with it, since it seemed the only sensible option. "Finn is my son."

What Angel was expecting was the awkward and terrified look most people got in their eyes when they heard he had a son. Not that Angel was a teen father or anything, but young singles in New York didn't tend to take kindly to the prospect of other people's kids. But Ryan just grinned at him.

"How old is he?"

"Five," Angel said, mouth quirking up.

"So, I have similar food tastes to a five year old." Ryan tipped his head back for a moment as if considering this. "I would say I'm embarrassed, but I'm really not."

Angel laughed, and the tightness in his chest from telling Ryan about Finn was gone, just like that. There was somehow absolutely no worry in his mind that Finn and Ryan would get along. That terrified him a little— that he was actually thinking about introducing this man to his son. This man could totally ruin him, and he probably would. *I'm fucked*, Angel thought, with a sense of inevitability. But he wouldn't, he swore he wouldn't, let this fuck up Finn.
***

"Do you want to come back to my place?" Angel asked softly as Ryan pulled on his jacket. The words were so gentle that Ryan could've missed them under the lazy throb of Eastern music that added ambiance to the restaurant. Ryan turned to Angel and raised an eyebrow.

"If you want," Angel amended, looking sheepish and more than a little hesitant, "I could drive you back to base in the morning. It would have to be before my son wakes up, but I wouldn't mind."

"Okay," Ryan responded quickly. He was more eager than he dared to let on, and he tried not to skip as he followed Angel to his car.

"I love this track," Ryan admitted when Angel turned the key in the ignition and Aman Jones immediately started playing.

"Me too," Angel replied, and Ryan watched as Angel's face broke into a grin without looking at him.

They chatted mindlessly about their jobs and what television shows they watched regularly. Ryan expounded on how much he loved some Danish crime drama that he couldn't get enough of. He just wanted to put his hand on the back of Angel's neck and kiss him when he nodded and smiled, seemingly understanding Ryan's little obsession. He resisted the urge because he didn't need an accident to put a hitch in their night.

They pulled into a spot behind a cute little apartment building and Ryan knew already, as he looked around, that he was starting to get too attached to this idea of a relationship with Angel. When they got inside the first door, Angel kissed him gently and twined their fingers together. It was a strange feeling, being kissed like that, casually and in semi-public, by someone Ryan actually genuinely wanted to kiss. Strange, but good, Ryan decided. He grinned at Angel and followed him up the flights of stairs to his apartment door.

"We're going to have to be quiet," Angel said, his voice low. "My sister's inside. She might have already crashed out on the couch, but she also might be awake still."

Angel looked a little worried, so Ryan, feeling bold, dropped a quick kiss on his lips. It was dry and over too fast, but Ryan hoped they'd have plenty of time to make up for that when they got inside. The corners of Angel's eyes crinkled, and he squeezed Ryan's hand before he unlocked the door.

Angel was in the process of pushing Ryan into the kitchen when a voice called out from the living room. There was a muffled conversation, and then Angel was back in the kitchen, grabbing Ryan's hand, and dragging him down the hallway.

Angel pulled him into what must have been the master bedroom, although it looked pretty small to Ryan. It seemed to contain about the usual amount of furniture for a non-military issue room: a queen-sized bed with a dark bedspread on it, a dresser, and two nightstands. Not that Ryan had much time or inclination to stand there appreciating the decor. Angel locked the door and immediately latched onto Ryan's shirt, pulling him in and kissing him more roughly than Ryan was quite ready for.

"I want you to fuck me," Angel whispered, when he pulled away from Ryan's lips and latched his mouth to the spot below his ear. Ryan shivered and felt himself immediately getting hard. He'd wanted this for years, and never quite dreamed of ever getting it, and now here he was, looming on the precipice of it. Ryan wasn't sure what the fuck he was meant to do, but luckily, Angel seemed to have taken over. Angel had turned nearly frantic, pushing Ryan's shirt off his shoulders and ripping off his own sweater. Ryan pulled his undershirt over his head and looked at Angel. He saw the tattoos on Angel's skin, and he hoped he'd have the chance— and the nerve— to trace them this time.

Angel was moving down to his jeans and Ryan let out a whimper. Angel's fingers assuredly unbuttoned and unzipped his pants as he shifted to lay open-mouthed kisses along Ryan's hip. He tugged down the jeans and, with them, Ryan's boxer-briefs. Now he needed Ryan to move, step out of them, and it seemed to jolt him momentarily out of his flurry of desperation. He looked up at Ryan, holding his eyes for a moment. When he leaned down again to engulf Ryan's dick with his mouth, Ryan shivered and pushed him away.

"If you want me to fuck you, you shouldn't. I'll cum too quickly," Ryan warned. Angel's answering grin was almost malevolent.

Angel removed his own pants quickly and pushed Ryan onto the bed. The next moment, Angel was on top of him, and Ryan found himself grappling to get his bearings and respond with as much finesse as Angel was, although he didn't think much of his chances. Then Angel reached across to the bedside table and pulled out a bottle of lube. When he squeezed out some onto his fingers and reached behind himself, Ryan had to squeeze his eyes shut, feeling his body ramping up absurdly at the sight— the *thought,* even— of what Angel was doing, fingering himself like that. Getting himself ready, for *Ryan.* Ryan drew in a deep breath, trying to calm himself, and opened his eyes to Angel straddling him, his head thrown back and his chest hitching with his breaths.

"I want to," Ryan ventured, helpless. His voice broke over the words, sounding wrecked even to his own ears, but his intent must have been clear, because Angel grinned at him with eyelids lowered and held out the lube.

Ryan covered his fingers and pressed two into Angel before he could lose his nerve, biting his lip as Angel's body opened for him easily, a low groan breaking from Angel's lips. It was the groan, more than anything, that made Ryan whimper and wrap his free hand around the base of his cock, fighting a heady rush of want that could have made coming too soon an unfortunate possibility. Above him, Angel was a sinuous bow of effort, and Ryan drew in a deep breath, moving his hand from his own dick to Angel's and marveling at the weight of it in his hand.

"Oh, fuck," Angel hissed through his teeth and grasped Ryan's wrist, stilling his hand. "Too much. I need you now before I cum all over your chest."

"Are you sure you're ready?" Now that the moment had arrived, Ryan's heart was pounding.

"Shut up," Angel gritted out, as he rolled a condom down Ryan's cock and guided it into him.

And just like that, they were joined. *Fucking.* Ryan was fucking a guy. He sounded out the thought verbally in his head, trying to comprehend the enormity of it. Angel felt so tight around him, and he suddenly couldn't believe he hadn't done this before. His fingers dug into Angel's hips, holding them down; he could tell Angel was itching to start moving, but he didn't know if there would be much more moving if

Angel started now. When he felt as ready as he'd ever be, he smacked at Angel's hip lightly, and he almost thought he'd done the wrong thing when Angel stuttered— until Angel caught his eyes with pupils blown black. Ryan's dick twitched reactively in the hot clutch of Angel's body, and let himself surrender to Angel's surge of energy as he set up a rolling rhythm that soon had Ryan's eyes rolling back in his head.

Despite his best efforts, this was still a first time for Ryan, a new feeling with intensity as much in his mind as in the overwhelming sensations. He felt the coil of his orgasm start soon enough, and reached down to Angel's leaking cock, wrapping his hand around it with the same pressure he usually put on his own. He figured that, if he liked it, Angel would too, and soon enough, Angel was proving that theory right, spurting onto Ryan's stomach. It was the sounds Angel made that undid Ryan at his core; he couldn't hold out any longer after Angel's last helpless groan, and came with a sharp cry.

Angel moved off him, tied off the condom, and threw it into the trash. Ryan barely had time to feel disappointment at the end of their encounter before Angel was crawling back over him, lapping the cum off Ryan's navel and then licking Ryan's mouth. The thought of tasting cum in a kiss had always perturbed him, but now, as he groaned helplessly into Angel's mouth, he couldn't recall why. Angel tasted salt-sour and dark, familiar and yet not, but it was the intimacy of it that made Ryan's gut fill with heat.

"Fuck," Ryan managed, when Angel pulled away at last to fall next to him.

"Yeah," Angel responded into his neck.

Ryan didn't remember falling asleep, but he woke up with one of Angel's legs draped over his hips and Angel's head on his shoulder. His arm was asleep and he didn't even care. He kissed Angel's forehead and felt the brush of long lashes as his eyes blinked open slowly, a small smile tugging at his lips. Angel kissed Ryan's chest, smoothed a hand up from his navel to his clavicle, and then shifted until he was half on top of Ryan.

Ryan had never thought much about how different it might be to be with another guy in terms of dynamics— he'd spent far too long trying not to think about it at all. When it did invade his thoughts, though, he supposed he'd imagined himself still in the commanding role that fell to him in his encounters with women. Now, though, with Angel, Ryan found himself enjoying the way Angel tended to take control, something completely unrelated to the positions they took in penetrative sex. He let Angel control this morning's make-out session and just enjoyed the way it felt. When Angel pulled away from Ryan's mouth and moved down his body, Ryan glanced at the clock and threw his head back.

"Fuck, we should stop," Ryan whined.

"Why?"

"We need to leave so you can get back here in time to get Finn to school and yourself to work."

"You remembered his name," Angel said, his voice softening, and Ryan laughed despite himself.

"Of course, I did."

Ryan couldn't quite interpret the look that passed over Angel's face, but from the way Angel kissed him afterward, he had to figure it couldn't mean anything bad. The kiss promised many more in the future, and in that moment, that was exactly what Ryan wanted.

Chapter Four

In the last five weeks, Angel had discovered that he really liked wrapping his body around Ryan after sex. He liked placing his face against the rigid pectoral muscle, sliding his fingers into the spaces between Ryan's ribs, hooking his ankle lazily around a calf. Ryan's breathing was rhythmic and soothing against Angel's cheek, and it was starting to become a real addiction.

"How was your trip home?" Angel asked Ryan, who was drawing lazy patterns on Angel's back in counterpoint to the gentle motions of Angel's fingers over Ryan's ribcage.

Ryan blinked slowly and his voice was rough with the first inklings of sleep. "It was good. My mom really liked 'Finn.' She actually cried. My sisters were so mad that my present was nine hundred times better than theirs. Not that my mom likes to play favorites, but I am definitely the favorite now."

Angel chuckled lightly and smiled up at Ryan, who was looking at him with warm, sleepy eyes. He kissed Ryan's chest. "I'm glad she liked it."

The next question came out of Angel's mouth apparently without permission from his brain: a stupid question, pointless. Angel felt pathetic as he felt the words pass his lips: "Did you tell them about us?" Especially when he knew the answer, when he knew that Ryan's career was so important to him. That a five-week relationship, that they hadn't even defined as such, was not important enough to risk everything Ryan had worked for since he was fifteen.

Ryan didn't answer. He just closed his eyes. At first, Angel thought Ryan was just going to ignore the question that was so clearly asking for a fight, but then Ryan whispered, "Have you told Finn about us?"

Angel wondered if he was too scared to let this happen. If he was asking for this fight because he didn't want Ryan to have any control over his life. There was a part of him that knew if he let Ryan in, Ryan would have a degree of control that Angel would rather not give up to anyone. He also knew, though, that this kind of clarity wasn't always available to Angel when it came to this relationship. Maybe he should grab onto it and run as fast as he could.

"See, we both have stuff that holds us back," Ryan reasoned, and for a moment, Angel hated him for being so logical. Ryan's hand was still tracing patterns on Angel's back, but it was more tentative now.

"This bar is killing my back," Ryan whined after a minute as he shifted, trying to cut the tension. The comment was blunt, but Angel took it in the spirit intended.

"We could go crawl into the loft," Angel murmured, kissing right above Ryan's nipple.

"I feel like a teenager, having to use your friend's place to get off."

"My apartment's just too far away, and we can't go to your place," Angel pointed out.

"You know I'm sorry about that," Ryan said, with a sigh. "You know I wish that was different."

"I actually don't," Angel returned, "because I don't know you all that well."

"Stop trying to push me away."

Angel shook his head as if he could shake off the comment. "Let's go up to the loft," he reiterated. *Drop it,* he tried to convey without words.

Ryan hummed in response and rolled off the bed. He wasn't nearly as spry as Angel would have assumed a soldier would be, his knees knocking loudly against the floor. Before they made their ascent, they both pulled on sweatpants in case Travis should come back from Mike's early.

They climbed up the narrow staircase and plopped into the blanket nest on top of the orthopedic mattress. Angel felt himself drifting quickly, wrapped around Ryan in Travis' decadent bed, until he heard his phone go off. He nearly fell down the steep steps scrambling to pick up the call. It was in the pocket of his chinos, tangled in cotton, and he got to it right before it went to voicemail.

"Hello?"

"Oh, thank goodness, you answered," his mom exhaled, and her voice was groggy and exhausted. It made his heart rate skyrocket.

"Is Finn okay?"

"Physically, he's fine, darling, but he woke up an hour ago. He won't stop crying and he's only asking for you. I can't get a coherent sentence out of him except that he wants his daddy."

Angel's chest clenched and he tasted the guilt in his mouth. He tried to swallow down the bitterness. Before he could ask to speak to Finn, Finn was sobbing into the phone. "Daddy? Daddy?"

Immediately, Angel felt like a monster. "Yeah, Finn, it's me."

The next sob wasn't as panic filled. Instead, it was drenched with relief. Angel wasn't sure that was much better. "I thought you'd left forever like mommy," Finn sobbed.

"Finn, I told you yesterday that I would come and get you tomorrow," Angel soothed, but the reminder didn't so much mollify his son as just renew the crying.

"But, but, I didn't know. I wasn't sure," Finn wept.

"I'm sorry, baby, I'm so sorry. I'll see you tomorrow."

"Come get me now," Finn demanded.

"I can't do that, Finn. I'm so far away right now. It would take me hours."

"That's okay, I can wait, but I need you to come, Daddy."

"Finn, I'm so sorry," Angel responded, and he nearly jumped out of his skin when Ryan's hands dropped onto his shoulders. Ryan squeezed his tense muscles, and Angel didn't want to feel better because of it. He didn't want to rely on it, but he leaned back anyway. It was just so easy.

"Daddy," Finn whined.

"Go get in your bed with the phone, and I'll sing you to sleep."

He heard a murmured conversation between Finn and his mom, and then Finn was clunking up the stairs to Angel's old bedroom.

"I still want you to come here."

"And I will tomorrow, but this is going to have to do for now."

There was a little whimper from the other side of the phone line, but Angel didn't say anything about it because it seemed resigned. He started singing instead, an old lyric his mom had sung for him and which he'd always used to lull Finn into slumber. He was pretty sure Finn was asleep after the first run through, but he sang the song once more. He could hear the hiccupped breathing from the other side of the line and he hung his head. He was clearly the worst dad in the history of dads. He was more worried about getting his rocks off than about his own flesh and blood.

"Thanks, darling." His mom's relieved voice drifted to his ear.

"I'm sorry."

"Oh, no, baby, I'm sorry; I just didn't know what to do. I'm sorry I called."

Angel sighed. "Mom, it's fine. He's my son."

"Don't start hating yourself, Angel," Mom said sternly. "Please, I'll feel horrible if you start beating yourself up because I couldn't calm down my grandson."

"It would never be your fault."

"It's not your fault either," she reasoned.

"That's debatable."

"Oh, Angel."

Angel scrubbed at his face with the heel of his hand. "I love you, Mom. I'll see you tomorrow."

"I love you too, sunshine."

Angel hung up the phone and took a deep, shaky breath. He felt, more than saw, Ryan drop down in front of him. He didn't know he was crying until Ryan wiped the tears off his cheeks.

"You're a good dad," Ryan declared after a few minutes of crouching down in front of Angel, one large, calming hand on his shoulder.

"You don't know that," Angel scoffed. "I could be a shit father and you would never know. You haven't even met him; there's no way you can say I'm a good dad."

Ryan threw him a wry look. "I know that, even at five, if I would've called my dad up crying, he would've told me to be a man and hung up on me. Or he just wouldn't have answered. And I know my dad loves me and he was a decent dad, but man, you're an amazing one. You just sang your son to sleep over the phone, which was beautiful."

Angel, feeling suddenly self-conscious, looked up at the ceiling and scrubbed at the stray tears still clinging to his lashes. "He's only five and his mom's dead; he's allowed to be sad."

"I didn't say he wasn't."

Angel looked up at Ryan, whose face was earnest. Angel kissed him suddenly, the gesture not sexy or loving but intensely, abruptly desperate.

***

Ryan wasn't expecting the teeth-clashing kiss from Angel, but he let him control it. Angel pushed Ryan into the wingback chair next to the couch and crawled on top of him, keeping the kisses erratic and fraught. Ryan put his hands on Angel's cheeks and tried to settle him down. Lately, their kisses had been more gentle and subtle; this was some first night shirt-ripping stuff. Ryan liked it and all, but he didn't like where it was coming from.

"Stop," Ryan said when Angel moved to suck at his neck, and Angel instantly moved away, jumping off Ryan as if he was all of a sudden disgusted or something. Ryan couldn't read him. He was slightly terrified that whatever was happening in this minute was relationship-defining, and he was in the dark about it.

Angel's features were cracking and Ryan couldn't stand it, couldn't watch it. He stood and pulled Angel into his shoulder. Ryan could feel the rushed, quivering breath that Angel released, and it made him flex his arms around him tighter.

"Come on, you need sleep," Ryan ordered, turning away from Angel but not before reaching for his hand. He dragged him up into the loft. Angel had gone pliant, and Ryan pulled him into the sleeping position he knew Angel liked the most. He wrapped Angel's limbs around himself, but Angel took the

69

liberty of pressing his face into Ryan's neck. Ryan didn't say anything when he felt wetness accompany Angel's shaky breaths. He just skimmed his fingers over his back and hoped that reassured Angel a little.

In the morning, Angel woke him up, which was such an irregularity that it made Ryan stiffen. He knew Angel was anxious to get home so he could go pick up Finn from his folks' place in Bedford, but it left a bad feeling in Ryan's gut. Angel made them scrambled eggs and toast, acting as if nothing was up. He placed a few kisses on Ryan's mouth as he was getting ready to leave and, as much as Ryan tried to dismiss the thought, he couldn't help thinking that they felt like a final goodbye.

Ryan took the subway back to base and the long ride let him think. When he was back in his apartment, he took a shower and then he texted Angel, asking him how Finn was. He didn't get a response, which wasn't highly unusual, but Ryan wanted to throw up or throw something nonetheless.

He resisted the urge to text Angel for the rest of the day. He had things to do, anyway. He went to the gym, did his laundry, made a few phone calls to his family, and Pete came over to watch the Sunday night baseball game on ESPN.

Throughout the entire game, Pete kept glancing over at him as if he had something to say, but wasn't sure how to voice it. Pete normally fixed all of his attention to the screen the entire time any baseball game was on, but he seemed oddly intent on Ryan this evening.

"Why didn't you tell me?" Pete asked suddenly, his voice a weird mixture of offended and curious.

Ryan blinked. "Tell you about what?"

"You and Angel."

For the second time that day, Ryan felt pure dread penetrate his veins. He glanced at Pete out of the corner of his eye, and he was shocked to find that Pete didn't look disgusted, just upset— as if the despondency wasn't due to Ryan's sexuality, but to the fact that he hadn't trusted Pete with it.

"I, uh," Ryan mumbled.

"Don't deny it," Pete began. "That'll just make me angrier, especially since I had to find out from fucking *Mike*."

Ryan just looked at Pete, shocked. Pete rarely raised his voice or got angry, and this was completely unexpected. But it seemed there was more to come.

"You know you were my friend first; there is no reason Mike should have known about you guys before me. That's a load of fucking bullshit, dude."

"I'm sorry," Ryan said helplessly.

"You should be," Pete snapped.

"It doesn't..." Ryan hesitated. "I thought it might bother you."

"That you like dudes?"

Ryan flinched. "Yeah."

"Have you met my oldest friend?" Pete demanded. "You know— the one that's banging some Broadway actor?"

Mike, of course. But Mike was *different,* Ryan thought helplessly, and sought for a way to articulate that. "It's just... it's just..."

"It's just what?" Pete demanded.

Ryan shrugged. " 'Don't ask, don't tell,' right?"

"You think I live by some archaic rule devised by the shitty US military?"

That put Ryan's back up despite himself. "Umm, well, since you're a part of the 'shitty US military,' yes?"

Pete rolled his eyes. "That's only because I like the adventure. I'm allowed to be critical of an organization I belong to. It's my prerogative as an American."

"So you don't care?" Ryan could hardly believe what he was hearing. It wasn't that he'd expected bigotry from Pete, but what happened on base had always seemed so separate from real life.

"Fuck no, but I do care that you didn't tell me. That hurts, man," Pete said, slapping the back of Ryan's head. Ryan winced, because when Pete slapped a guy, he held nothing back.

"Well, *that* hurt, so I guess we're even," Ryan suggested, but Pete snorted.

"Not even close, fucker."

Pete pulled him into a long hug when he left and promised Ryan again that he didn't care about who Ryan liked, so long as he knew before Mike next time. At least one of Ryan's concerns had been solved. He thought about trying to solve the other one, but he fell asleep with his phone on his chest still waiting for a response.

The rest of the week went by much like Sunday. Ryan texted and called Angel with no responses. He tried to extract information out of Travis through Mike, but Mike told him Travis was mum on the subject of Angel and Finn, though Mike did tell him that Travis had been spending more of his time with them. Ryan couldn't take it. He felt out of mind with worry and what he didn't want to acknowledge was heartbreak. His commanding officer kept throwing him pointed looks, and Ryan tried valiantly to pull it together, but he hated the feeling that, without Angel, all he had left was the military and its rigid rules.

It was Friday when he found out that his unit was shipping out at the end of the month. This time, it was a tour in Iraq that meant fifteen months away. He called his parents and his mom cried while his dad expressed how proud he was of Ryan. Then, Ryan tried again to call Angel, but he still wasn't answering. Ryan wondered if he should just take the tour and use it to let himself forget about the man he knew he could fall for.

It only took him thirty minutes to decide that wasn't an option. He went outside and it was pouring; he pulled his hood up and walked to the subway. It took three different trains and over an hour to get to Angel's place. When he finally got to Angel's building, he was drenched. He pressed the buzzer and the door hummed as it unlocked. He walked up to the apartment door and knocked.

Angel opened the door with money in his hand, mouth falling open when he saw Ryan and not the delivery man. They stared at each other until there appeared a little face pressing in between Angel's leg and the door.

"Hi," Finn said, and Angel looked down on him with a confused look on his face.

"Hello," Ryan responded softly.

"Who are you?"

"I'm Ryan."

"Ryan." Finn tested it out. "Did you bring us dinner?"

"No, I... um..." Ryan floundered, looking desperately at Angel.

"He's my friend," Angel told Finn.

"Oh," Finn said, and then after a little contemplation asked, "Do you want to stay for dinner?"

"Um, I'm not sure your dad would be okay with that."

"Daddy?" Finn inquired, looking up at Angel with a furrowed brow.

"No, Ryan, come on in. We ordered pizza, and I always order extra because *someone* likes to eat cold pizza more than he likes to eat warm pizza."

"Daddy," Finn whined. "Ryan, do you want to watch cowboy movies with us?"

"I love cowboy movies," Ryan said, not entirely untruthfully. "They're my favorite kind."

"Me too," Finn agreed, grabbing Ryan's hand and dragging him to the living room. "Look, I have all the toys." Finn showed him his large collection of little plastic cowboys and horses, his pretend holster, and his sheriff star pin.

"I'm impressed," Ryan said, and Finn grinned. The grin was so reminiscent of Angel that Ryan's answering smile was slightly wistful.

"Sorry to steal your new friend, kid, but I think Ryan needs to change before he catches a horrible cold," Angel said to Finn, handing Ryan a stack of clothes. Ryan went to the bathroom and put on the sweatpants and t-shirt. They were a little snug, but they smelled like Angel, so Ryan didn't care.

The door buzzed again, and this time it was the pizza delivery man. Angel brought the box into the small kitchen and called them in. Finn zoomed into the kitchen and Ryan followed him. As soon as Angel filled a plate for him, Finn zipped back out of the room.

"Why are you here?" Angel cut right to the chase.

"Because you've been ignoring me."

"That wasn't a sign for you?"

"Do you want me to leave?"

Angel sighed. "Finn will be confused if you just leave."

"He's five, Angel; I'm sure he'll get over it after a few minutes."

"You don't understand," Angel said, avoiding Ryan's eye. "I've never seen him talk to a stranger so much in his life, much less offer to watch a movie with him and show him his toys. He likes you."

Ryan was confused. "Isn't that a good thing?"

"I don't know if I can do this."

"Why not?"

"Because you're in the closet, and I can't have the person I'm dating being ashamed of us. I refuse to explain that to Finn."

"I'm not ashamed," Ryan protested.

"You might as well be."

"That's not fair."

"Daddy, Ryan," Finn called from the living room, "I want to watch the movie."

Angel threw Ryan a look, and then shrugged. "Let's go before the pizza gets cold. I don't like cold pizza like my son does."

Finn hit play the minute they sat down, and Ryan smiled at the way Finn sat enraptured at the coffee table, his eyes glued to the screen. Ryan was impressed that Finn could stare at the TV and not miss his mouth when he took a bite of pizza or picked up his glass to drink his apple juice.

When they all finished eating, Angel grabbed the plates and took them to the kitchen. Finn stayed sitting like a pretzel at the coffee table, and instead of eating, he played absentmindedly with his toys until Angel came back and ruffled his hair. He sat next to Ryan again and Ryan turned to grin at him. After a moment, Angel's lips turned up at the corner.

Ryan went back to watching the screen and nearly jumped out of his skin when Angel laid a hand on his thigh. He looked at him questioningly, and Angel's features were soft and unguarded. Ryan put his arm on the back of the couch behind Angel's head.

It was as if they were moving in slow motion. After a few minutes, Angel leaned his head against Ryan's shoulder. Then, minutes later, Ryan dropped his arm to Angel's shoulder. The movie ended and Finn turned to them. Ryan tensed a little, but Angel didn't pull away and kept a steady hand on Ryan's thigh. Finn just tilted his head for an instant, but then beamed and climbed into Angel's lap.

"What was your favorite part?" Finn asked Ryan.

"I love it when they're at the gas station."

"That's Daddy's favorite part, too."

Ryan looked at Angel, and Angel nodded before telling Finn, "It's bedtime."

Finn sighed, but headed towards his room dutifully, grabbing the sheriff star off the table. When Finn was out of sight, Angel grabbed the back of Ryan's neck and kissed him. Ryan's apprehension bled out of him as Angel's tongue pressed against his lips. Angel tasted like oregano and citrus soda, with an undertone of the chai tea he favored.

"I missed you," Angel whispered onto Ryan's lips.

"Missed you too."

"Daddy, come read me a story," Finn called from his room.

Angel got up and Ryan dropped his head onto the back of the couch. He tried to get the bilious feeling in his stomach to calm, because he now had to tell Angel the real reason he came. After this timidly domestic evening, this night that was so easy and was the next stop on their rickety relationship train, he was going to have to tell Angel that he was leaving in two weeks.

"Goodnight, Ryan," Finn said, darting back into the living room and waving.

"Night, buddy," Ryan waved back.

A few minutes after Finn ran back to his bedroom, Angel was back on the couch, curled under Ryan's arm. Angel was flicking through the channels, looking for something to catch his attention. He settled on a John Hughes marathon.

"Angel, I have something else to tell you," Ryan declared, clearing his throat. Angel mumbled into Ryan's side. "It's kind of serious," he added. Angel looked up at him and his eyes were soft and tentatively alarmed.

"What?"

"I'm deploying in two weeks."

Chapter Five

Angel felt his mouth fill with the rancid taste of partially digested pizza. He swallowed, and it burned when it returned to his stomach. He wanted very much to either punch Ryan or cry or wake up. He'd prefer just waking up. His next thought was that he's a colossal idiot. He should have never have let this man into his life, into his son's life.

"Repeat that," Angel ordered, pulling away.

"I'm deploying in two weeks."

"For how long? To where?"

"Fifteen months. Iraq."

"Are you fucking shitting me?"

Ryan shrugged. "I understand that this is horrible timing, but I don't really get to make decisions about my deployment."

"No, I really don't think you understand," Angel snapped.

"It's not like I'm asking for a commitment here," Ryan mumbled. His face showed genuine confusion and pain. Angel's fingers ached to run over his scalp and clutch his neck comfortingly, but Angel also wanted to punch him because he didn't understand at all. It was both a relief and a headache.

"It's not about a commitment," Angel snarled. His own response made him grimace, but he couldn't stop, because Ryan needed to understand what else he was doing. "You just let me show this relationship to my son, knowing that you'd be leaving. And not only that, but to go to Iraq, of all fucking places."

Ryan sighed. "I know that was selfish, but it was only one day. He'll forget about me. He's only five."

"You honestly don't get it, do you?"

"Angel," Ryan pleaded.

"Do you know that he asks me if I'm going to leave like his mom and never come back? He wonders it when I go to the grocery store or work or to go fuck you. And sometimes, he calls me in the middle of the night because he thinks I'm dead and that he's an orphan. But I'm not the only one he wonders that about. He wonders it about his grandparents, his aunts and uncles, his cousins, his babysitter, his friends, his teachers, and people he just met. He's had this tragic loss and he's only five. He's terrified of death. You could die, Ryan. You realize that, don't you?"

Ryan had drawn his lips in between his teeth. Angel flinched at the vulnerability and dread stamped on Ryan's face, and he watched as Ryan's eyes became damp. Angel knew he was hiding his emotions well because Ryan looked down and shook his head. "Maybe he's not the only one who's terrified."

"What does that mean?"

"Maybe you're terrified too. Maybe his mom's death terrified you as well."

"And death doesn't terrify you?" Angel scoffed, crossing his arms defensively, because maybe he had been projecting his emotions and reservations onto Finn, but he didn't want to be told so by Ryan. Maybe his son would be okay if Ryan left; he just didn't want to find out. He didn't want to have to see his son gloomier or more petrified than he already was and had been.

"It's why I came here, but maybe that was a stupid idea," Ryan responded, rubbing the back of his neck and getting off the couch. He was nearly at the front door before Angel reacted. But when Angel did, it was with a fumbled dash that ended in him plowing unceremoniously into Ryan's back. Ryan steadied him with a miserable look on his face.

"What did you say?"

"It was a stupid idea?" Ryan asked.

"No, no."

"Don't make me say it again."

"Say it, please," Angel begged, "just say it again."

"It's why I came here. I came here because I'm terrified. I'm terrified of losing this. I'm terrified of dying."

***

Angel was just looking at him. He squinted his eyes at Ryan, little lines appearing next to them. It was calculating, and it made Ryan squirm. He wanted very much to turn away, but he knew Angel would respect him more if he withstood the scrutiny.

"I'm glad it's not just me," Angel said, putting his hands on Ryan's neck and pressing their foreheads together. Ryan's hands moved to the back of Angel's neck. Angel kissed him, and it was the gentlest kiss Ryan had ever been a part of.

"I'm sorry about Finn," Ryan murmured when Angel pulled away.

"I know."

"He's wonderful, by the way."

Angel closed his eyes with a longing smile on his face. "Two weeks, you said."

"Yeah, I have them off. I would usually go home, but I was just there, and my parents are leaving for vacation this weekend. My sisters are going to come for a visit next week. And when I thought about the time off, I just really wanted to spend it with you."

"Stop," Angel said softly.

"Stop what?"

"Stop making this more difficult."

"How am I making this more difficult?" Ryan furrowed his brow.

"By being so fucking sincere and quixotic."

"Sometimes, I have no idea what you're saying. But will you confuse me next week, and the one after?"

That made Angel laugh. "Sure, but we are going to need to make a plan."

"Can we do that next week?"

"Sure."

"Right now," Ryan said, "I want you to wrap around me. I haven't slept well since last time."

"Stop making me miss you already."

Ryan giggled, an honest to God giggle that would get him teased until next week if Pete heard it. Angel smiled, and Ryan needed to touch him more. He wrapped his arms around Angel, and they stumbled to Angel's bedroom. They both stripped down to their boxer-briefs. Angel intertwined their legs and kissed Ryan's shoulder. Ryan ran his fingers through Angel's hair and fell asleep quickly, contented.

***

Angel woke up sleep-warm and well-rested, his hand on Ryan's hip and Ryan's hand in his hair. He never slept like this with Alicia. Alicia had always wrapped herself tightly in a blanket; in fact, they'd always had their own blankets on their sides of the bed. When they'd moved in together after finding out she was pregnant, she had demanded they get a king size bed because he drove her crazy with his clinging. It had taken months to pay off, and it engulfed the entirety of their small bedroom. It had been so big that Angel had to screw shelves into the wall for pseudo-bedside tables and side step to bed every night. It had caused additional problems when they had to move their dresser into the living room when Finn was born, and his crib and the dresser wouldn't fit together. After years with Alicia, he never thought he would want to sleep this closely with anyone again, except maybe for Travis. But here he was, tangled up with this hard-muscled man who shouldn't be cuddly at all.

He could hear Finn moving around in the living room, probably playing with his toys or watching cartoons. He'd want breakfast soon. Angel tried to extricate himself from Ryan's hold without waking him, and he nearly managed it. But he couldn't help running a hand over Ryan's head, and that caused Ryan's eyes to flutter open sluggishly.

"Morning," Ryan roughed out. He cleared his throat and smiled.

"Good morning. I'm going to go make breakfast for Finn."

Panic showed clearly on Ryan's face, and Angel felt his own terror intensify. He never had to worry about this kind of terror with Alicia. He wondered if this was too much— if last night, there was a weird haze that was now burning off. If Ryan had realized his disastrous mistake, Angel didn't know if he'd recover.

"I should've set an alarm," Ryan groused.

Relief flooded Angel with a devastating need to either laugh or cry. Instead, he smiled and ran his hand over Ryan's scalp again. Ryan grabbed his hand before he could pull it away and tugged him onto the bed. Angel face-planted into Ryan's side, not at all gracefully, but Ryan didn't seem to mind as he hauled him up for a kiss. Angel felt his cock stir when Ryan yanked on his hair as his tongue delved into Angel's mouth. The thing that really got Angel was that there wasn't much to be attracted to in this moment. He was lying at a weird angle that caused an aching in his spine, and they both had intense morning breath, but Angel still wanted nothing more than to stay right there. He knew they could probably get away with it, too. Finn was a patient kid, but Angel also knew that nine-thirty was breakfast time on the weekends, and it was already nine twenty-five. It wouldn't be fair to make Finn wait much longer.

"As much as I want to stay in bed with you all day, I need to go do parent things."

"Mmmkay," Ryan agreed, his eyes closing. Angel thought he was going back to sleep, so he turned to put on some lounge clothes and make breakfast. He was surprised to feel Ryan press against his back, but not as surprised as when Ryan's hard cock pressed against his ass. "Guess I'll just go take care of this in the shower."

"Fuck," Angel groaned as Ryan thrust lightly against him. "Maybe a quick blow job."

Angel didn't need to look to know Ryan had that dopey look on his face. He turned and dropped to his knees. He didn't tease, just tongued at the head of Ryan's cock, and then took it into his mouth in one motion.

It didn't take long. Ryan thrust shallowly, and Angel hollowed his cheeks, swallowing rhythmically until Ryan groaned and came. Angel kissed Ryan's thighs and smiled at him as he stood.

He went to open the door, but Ryan covered his hand, turned him around, and dropped to his knees in front of Angel. Angel felt his heart beating and it trapped the air in his chest. Ryan had never initiated like this before, and his fingers shook as he kissed from Angel's navel down to the thick bulge of his cock, peeling the underwear aside. Ryan licked hesitantly, and Angel placed his hands on Ryan's shoulders in what he hoped was a comforting gesture. Ryan looked pleased, wrapping his lips around the tip, and Angel didn't think it would take much for him to cum. He closed his eyes as Ryan licked and sucked. He didn't realize his hips were moving until he heard Ryan sputtering.

"Fuck, Ryan, I'm sorry," Angel panted. Ryan looked up at him, and Angel was a little surprised to see timid arousal in his eyes. A moment later, Ryan grabbed his hips and pulled him in closer, and Angel came undone at that. When Ryan pulled away, he looked enormously pleased with himself. He stood up and Angel dragged him in for a kiss, sloppy and earnest. Angel wanted nothing more than to crawl back into bed and spend the rest of the day there, pushing Ryan as far as he would go. Angel was an arm's reach away from heaving Ryan back into bed when a light rap sounded on the door.

"Daddy, you said we could go to the zoo today," Finn called softly, "and I'm really hungry."

"I'm coming, kiddo," Angel responded. Then, "Want to go to the zoo?" he asked Ryan, placing a peck on his lips.

"Absolutely."

Angel went to the kitchen to get breakfast started while Ryan headed to the bathroom to take a shower. Angel was cutting up a banana for Finn's pancakes when Finn came in looking superbly concerned.

"What's wrong, kiddo?"

"The shower's on, but you're in here and I'm right here. Is it a burglar or a ghost?"

"Well, wouldn't it be silly for a burglar to let us know he or she is here? And a ghost probably doesn't need a shower."

"Who is it, then?" Finn asked impatiently.

"It's Ryan."

Finn seemed pleased with this response, and his eyes searched Angel's face. Angel felt uncomfortable under his son's scrutiny, which was absolutely ridiculous, because he was twenty-seven and Finn was only five. It was just that this little person's opinion was the one that mattered most to Angel.

Finn seated himself at the counter and grabbed a slice of banana off the cutting board. He kept looking at Angel as if to measure him up. Angel found himself doing anything to get away from those eyes, the only visible trait reminiscent of Alicia. Finn hummed knowingly like Angel's mom always did.

"Is he coming to the zoo with us?"

"If you want me to," Ryan said, walking into the kitchen, droplets of water still visible in his buzz cut.

"Have you ever been to the Queens Zoo?"

"No, I don't think I have."

Finn let out an enthusiastic squeal and jumped around the kitchen. "I go all the time; I can show you around."

Ryan grinned at Finn and then sent a furtive glance to Angel. Angel winked at him, and Ryan scrunched his face in what Angel assumed was supposed to be a returning wink. He chuckled happily as he poured the batter onto the skillet.

***

Ryan was set to leave in two days. He only had two days left. This was his second tour, and yet, his nerves were far more uptight this time. He knew it was because this time, he had something to stay in the States for— something far more important to him than loyalty to his country, but the thing was, he *was* loyal. He'd do his job because it's what he signed up for, and the Army had done a lot for him over the years.

He had been bullied a lot as a kid. It was never anything precise because there hadn't been much to bully. Maybe that had been the problem: He wasn't specifically smart or athletic or unattractive, but he had been specifically sweet. If there was one thing middle-schoolers and high-schoolers hated, it was sweetness. He had joined JROTC for something to do, something to forget the names he was called, and maybe to have people to hang out with at lunch. He had found that and more when he got buff, and the result was that the bullying had stopped. His high school days went from miserable to bearable, and that was all thanks to the US military. He felt a loyalty to the Army because it had saved his life, and he wanted to repay that if he could by protecting others.

It was just that now, it was ruining his life. The last week and a half had been idyllically domestic; he had spent more time in bed and picking up toys than he had any other time in his life. While some people might find home life excruciatingly boring, Ryan wanted to drown in it. He had introduced Angel to his sisters, and it had gone better than he ever imagined.

Ruth had gotten this sad smile on her face and almost started crying. Nicola had pulled Angel to the side and lectured him until Finn saved Angel with his long description of their trip to the Queens Zoo. Angel and his sisters had ended up chatting like old friends, and Ryan had felt a little bit left out.

Currently, Angel was tracing Ryan's abs with his index finger, and Ryan felt the involuntary contractions that were making Angel smirk. He wished he could put this supple, teasing Angel in his pocket and bring him out when he was lying on the cot in Bumfuck, Iraq, hoping to hell his team made it to their destination through bomb-riddled routes and that the hours would move faster, closer to home. Of course he'd discovered this now, the first person who could push him out of his comfort zone. It was just Ryan's luck.

"Will you promise to give me a chance when I get back?" Ryan sighed into Angel's downy locks.

"What are you talking about?" Angel demanded, pulling away to make eye contact with Ryan.

"I don't want you to promise you'll wait for me. I don't want you to make a commitment to me. I just want a chance in fifteen months."

"I actually don't understand you," Angel said.

"I don't want a promise because fifteen months is a really long time and..."

"And you think I'm a cheater," Angel lamented, swinging his leg over the edge of the bed.

"No, no, it's not that, Angel, it's really not. It's just..."

"What? Explain it to me. Dig yourself out of this hole."

Ryan sighed. "I won't be able to communicate with you like other soldiers and their significant others. It will only be innocuous emails because Skype is reserved for families and wives. You'll start to resent me, and I won't be able to come home knowing that. I just want a chance. I want you to date other people, and when I come back, I want a chance. I can't change the US military, but I can let you back out, at least for a while."

"What if I don't want out?"

"That's fine, but if you ever start resenting me, I want you to go out and do something about it without feeling guilty like you're cheating. Because you're not a cheater. I don't want you to be angry when I come back. I want to see you smile."

"Okay," Angel said slowly, "but I don't like this."

"I understand."

The next morning, Ryan woke up early, nuzzling Angel awake. Ryan traced every one of Angel's tattoos with either his tongue or fingertips. They rocked smoothly together and, unlike that morning three weeks before, it didn't feel like a goodbye, even though it should. It felt like a promise that Ryan didn't want.

Chapter Six

It was soft kisses and closed eyes with disheartened smiles that morning. Angel pressed his hands under Ryan's shirt and his face into the crook of his neck while Ryan placated him with his melodic hums. Angel made banana pancakes and kissed Ryan with syrup and powdered sugar on their tongues. Finn sat quietly at the table, and while that wouldn't usually concern Angel, Ryan brought out a loquacious side of Finn that was missing this final morning. Ryan had his fingers threaded through Angel's. Their hands rested between their plates, and Finn glanced at them every so often. Occasionally, he made a disconcerted sound but continued eating.

"Are you going to come back?" Finn asked finally, dragging the last piece of pancake through his syrup puddle.

"I hope so," Ryan responded honestly.

"But you might not?"

"Well, it is more dangerous than most situations."

"But you're going to be careful?"

"Of course."

"Can I send you letters and pictures?"

Ryan smiled. "I would love that."

"So we could be pen pals?"

"Yeah, bud, I'd like that."

"'Kay."

Ryan grinned at him, and an almost imperceptible smile appeared on Finn's face. Ryan stood up and ruffled Finn's hair as he took his dishes to the sink. The smile got bigger, and when Ryan opened his arms, Finn jumped into them, nearly knocking the plate out of Ryan's hand. He didn't cry, but he did take deep breaths that shook a little on the inhale. Ryan closed his eyes, looking pained.

Angel really wished he could understand this connection they seemed to have with Ryan. It was as if something had tied them together from the moment they met, but Angel didn't really believe in fate. He didn't want to be the heroine of some lust-covered romance novel, but he felt an undeniable connection to Ryan that his son seemed to feel too.

As Ryan was getting ready to leave, Finn skittered off to his bedroom, and Angel wondered if it might be too much for him to handle. Ryan looked a bit put out, but didn't say anything. Instead, he took the opportunity to kiss Angel, and every time he pulled away, Angel leaned in for another, because eventually, one would be the last.

Ryan was nearly out the door when Finn plowed into him with a strangled yelp, waving his arms and shouting nonsensically. Ryan hoisted him into his arms, and Finn bravely gave Ryan his best smile.

"What's wrong, bud?"

"I had to find it."

"What?"

"My sheriff badge. It'll protect you" he explained, thrusting the little plastic star into Ryan's hand.

Angel knew how much that toy meant to Finn; it was part of a set Alicia's parents gave him before they moved. He kept it by his bed at all times, and Angel didn't realize there were tears on his face until both Ryan and Finn were staring at him. Ryan pulled him in to his side, and Angel went willingly.

"Thanks, bud," Ryan said, kissing the crown of Finn's head. He kissed Angel in the exact same place, and then squeezed them both close one last time. With a small wave, Ryan slipped out the door.

"He's going to come back, right?" Finn asked.

"I hope so," Angel responded.

***

The first month was awful. Finn asked Angel a lot of questions about the military and the war, and Angel didn't get any response to his e-mails. Even though letters arrived for Finn every few weeks, Angel got radio silence and longing, a longing built on not enough time and the memory of sweet words, soft touches, and hot kisses.

It got better when Finn went on summer break. There was a flurry of activity around the apartment, and Angel didn't have to think about the fact that Ryan barely responded to his e-mails, and when he did, it was half-hearted. He could focus on all the excursions Finn wanted to go on and the games he wanted to play. He made a deal with Rosa to be Finn's summer nanny for room and board and five hundred dollars. She commandeered his bedroom, which honestly helped remove some of the longing, and he ended up on Finn's trundle bed. The one-on-one attention from Rosa was exactly what Finn needed, and even though he sent letters and pictures regularly to Ryan, he didn't seem sad or scared about it.

In mid-July, Angel went out with Mike and Travis to a bar that Mike's friend worked at. He was probably way too many beers in, and he should've just leaned against Travis until it wore off a little. Of course, that's not what he did; instead, when a girl in a mini dress and fuck-me heels brushed against him while reaching to get the martini she ordered, he grinned at her. They chatted about the most inane shit Angel could think of because all he really wanted was those bee-stung lips around his cock. He waited a good fifteen minutes before asking her.

"Wanna blow me in the bathroom?"

She sucked in a sharp breath, but nodded.

They stumbled to the bathroom, and Angel locked the door behind them. She got right to work, unbuttoning his pants and pulling them down with his boxers. She was a fucking expert at this, but looking down at her, Angel almost went flaccid when he thought about how her expert tongue had nothing on Ryan's stumbling enthusiasm. He looked away and thought of nothing until he came in her mouth; then, she walked to the sink and spat, almost delicately, into it. She kissed him as he pulled up his pants. Her mouth tasted like him, vodka, and something sweet, and he hated it. She brought his hand down between her legs, and he let her guide him until she was humming against his lips and quivering against his fingers. He'd loved this once, but now, it felt automatic, and he was furious, suddenly and unfairly, with her and with Ryan. She went to say something, but he washed his hands and walked out, leaving her stunned.

She wasn't the only one. Travis was still sitting at the bar with Mike, his face pinched in a judgmental expression. Travis made eye contact with him and the scorn hurt; Angel flipped Travis off and kept walking out of the bar.

He took a cab home, and the fare was astronomical. He had to pound on the door because Rosa had put the chain on, not expecting him home tonight, and her cell phone was turned off. She finally came to the door in sleep-mussed clothes, brandishing a knife, which struck him as hilarious in his drunken state. She seemed less amused. She put the knife down and shoved him until his back smacked hard into the door frame.

"What was that for?" he yelled indignantly.

"Ryan and Finn," she hissed. "You're a mess, Angel!"

"Whatever," he responded, the wind knocked out of him. "I'm going to bed."

"You go in that room, and I will murder you. Sleep on the couch, you disgusting fuck."

"I'll do whatever the fuck I want."

"You go in there, and your son will be scared. You're a fucked S.O.B if you subject him to that."

He turned away from her and tried not to sprint to the bathroom. Her words replayed in his mind as he vomited the contents of his stomach into the toilet. When he was sure there was nothing left to throw up, he climbed slowly to his feet and brushed his teeth. He rifled through the linen closet for a blanket, found Alicia's old quilt from college, and threw that on the couch. He poured some water and forced himself to drink it before passing out on the couch.

A few hours later, Finn was poking him awake. He blinked, and his head screamed while his stomach roiled. Finn looked perturbed.

"Daddy, you're taking up the whole couch, and I want to watch cartoons."

"Sorry," he croaked.

"Are you sick?"

"You could say that."

"Gramma always says you should sleep when you're sick."

"That's probably a good idea," he responded, as he dragged himself to Finn's room.

His sister was not so gentle when she woke him up two hours later. She was making an awful racket with the cymbals she bought Finn as a joke one year— a cruel, horrible joke.

"You are a fuck," she told him succinctly.

"Fuck off."

"Travis texted me because, even though you're a big prick, he still wanted to make sure you got home. He also told me what you did, and you are a fuck." She yanked the covers off him. He rolled over so his face was pressed into the pillow and flipped her off. Not that he disagreed with her; he just didn't like having his nose rubbed in it.

Travis didn't respond to his texts or talk to him until Finn's birthday party, where Travis and Mike both gave him the most condemnatory looks as they shoved their gifts into his hands at the door. Travis' face immediately switched as Finn threw himself into Travis' arms, introducing him to his friends. Mike took longer to drop his bitch face, and Angel realized that Mike was burning holes into the presents with his eyes. The first had Travis' scrawl on it. It was addressed to Finn, of course, and signed from both Travis and Mike. Angel set it on the birthday table and looked down at the second present before the note made him almost drop it like a sizzling coal. It wasn't Ryan's handwriting— it must be Mike's— but it was signed from Ryan. He turned to look at Mike, who blew air out of his nose in a sardonic laugh.

Angel had to rush to the bathroom. He slammed the door closed and splashed water on his face. He wanted to end the party, curl up in his own bed, put on the sweatshirt Ryan left, and wallow. He didn't, of course, but he splashed the water onto his face a few more times just to be sure no tears would leak out of his eyes. He rejoined the party, and it made him feel better to see concern flash across Travis' features.

The party was good, and Finn had an amazing time. He squealed in delight at Ryan's present: a stack of DVDs and a cowboy hat. When most of his guests had left, Finn made Angel and Travis play Monopoly with him, but Mike had to leave for a shift at the restaurant. Before bed, they watched a DVD, and Finn told Angel in a sleepy haze that he missed Ryan. Angel didn't miss the sad look Travis threw him at that.

Angel tried to convince himself not to be jealous of Finn's communication with Ryan, but he still was. His son got regular letters and mentions in Ryan's e-mails. Angel felt like an idiot being jealous of a five-year-old, but he couldn't help it. He sent a birthday card to Ryan in August and got a simple thank you letter in response.

Finn and Rosa went back to school in the beginning of September, Travis and Mike moved in together after Travis' lease was up, and Angel sunk a little deeper into his funk. Finn was busy almost constantly, and so happy that Angel didn't want to bring him down, so he put on a show that took every ounce of his energy. Everybody was so immersed in what they were doing, and Angel felt like he was just waiting around. He had a show in Manhattan in late September, at least. Travis invited him to crash on their couch, and he accepted.

They went out that night; mainly, Angel thought, because they didn't want to spend time alone with his depressed ass. Mike wanted to go dancing, so they ended up at a club near their apartment. To dance, Angel needed to drink, which wasn't hard, because that's how he'd been forgetting, anyway. Seven beers in, he was starting to tilt when he walked. When hands fixed onto his hips, he didn't pull away. He just swayed along.

"Come on, let's go," Travis yelled over the bass. He was angry, if his eyebrows were any indication, but Angel didn't care.

"He's good," said the burly dude whose hands sat possessively on Angel's hips.

"He's anything but good," Travis hissed back. His tone was livid, and for some reason Angel liked that.

"No, I'm good," Angel said, and leaned back to kiss the guy.

Travis' jaw clicked closed and Angel smirked back. He turned around and pressed his groin to the guy's. For all practical purposes, they were dry-humping; in response, Travis huffed off. Because he couldn't think of anything better, Angel went home with the guy and let him fuck him into the mattress. The guy didn't even seem to care if Angel got off, and Angel had to tug himself off before pulling on his clothes. He left right after and took the subway home. It kind of felt like he had a death wish, and he was thankful no one was at his place; Finn was safe at his parents'.

Travis didn't speak to him again until October. He'd promised Finn a trip to the zoo before it got too cold. Angel was outside, smoking a cigarette, when Travis arrived. Travis literally smacked the cigarette out of his lips and glared at him.

"What the fuck? Seriously, what the fuck?" Travis screamed in his face, and Angel almost told him to be quiet, but the yelling was at least making him feel something.

"What the fuck is with you? I'm just having a smoke."

"You've barely smoked since Finn was born, and you vowed after Alicia that you would quit completely."

"I did."

"I know; that's where my fucking problem lies."

"Sometimes, I just need one."

"You need to stop being a whiny fuck and admit you miss him. Don't go leaving your son an orphan because you're emotionally constipated."

Angel snorted. "If I'm emotionally constipated, I'm not the only one. I've just been following his lead."

"What are you talking about? What about the letter Mike gave you at Finn's party?"

"What are you talking about?" Angel asked incredulously.

"The letter Mike was supposed to give you at Finn's party."

"He never gave me anything," Angel said, now superbly confused.

That did it. Travis was abruptly so angry he could barely scroll through his contacts to call Mike; he walked away to conduct a whispered yelling match. Travis' face when he looked back at Angel had so much remorse, but Angel really didn't care. He just wanted his letter.

They went upstairs and, when Mike arrived, he looked petulant. Travis wouldn't make eye contact with him. Angel could understand why, but as mad as he was at Mike, he didn't want this to break apart their relationship. Travis was so happy these days. When Travis told Mike to leave, though, Angel didn't stop him.

Then he read the letter, and it was as if the words were stitching up his heart.

***

Ryan wondered if his letter to Angel got lost, removed from Mike's letter, if Mike didn't understand what he was supposed to do with it, if Mike hadn't given it to him, or, worse, if Angel didn't really care anymore. He didn't think it was the worst, or really, he had to hope it wasn't, because then why would Angel keep up the innocuous e-mails and letters and cards? Surely, he just hadn't seen it.

The mail was also sporadic, so maybe the response got lost somewhere on its long journey. He wouldn't be getting mail now for a while. They were in transit and communication between units on the ground was rough, not to mention communication home.

He had to keep himself busy to keep from being miserable, so when they were on base, he played soccer with Pete in their makeshift camps or cards with the rest of the guys. Pete and his constant smiles kept everyone's spirits up, and his own countdown helped Ryan focus.

These had been the longest months of his life, and the only thing keeping him from wallowing in his sadness was the star he kept in his left breast pocket, and Angel's worn blue shirt that he wore to bed.

He was lying on his cot now, toying with the star and smiling. He knew Finn liked his gifts; Finn and Angel had reported that. He itched to curl up on the worn sofa with those two right now. He didn't want the combat, even though he used to live for it: He wanted domesticity. Tomorrow, they'd head into one of the most dangerous areas on their route. They'd been warned about the car bombs; Ryan's CO wanted him to drive. He didn't want to think about his reality. He closed his eyes and imagined himself home, not in the middle of the desert.

The next morning, most of the trip went off without a hitch. They were almost in the safety zone when it happened. Ryan had an inkling that something was wrong before his mind even realized the cause. The beat up sedan to the side of them was not filled with people. It was full of dummies and one bomber in the driver's seat. Ryan swerved and punched the accelerator.

Chapter Seven

Angel loved Travis, he really did, but he could be such a pain in the ass. Heartbroken Travis was even worse. When Angel offered to let Travis stay with them until he could figure out what to do, he thought Travis would spend one night, tops three, bitching about Mike, but then go back to their apartment in Chelsea. It had been a week, and Travis' constant presence was putting a strain on Angel and Finn. Travis wavered between bitching, solemn sniffling, and running about maniacally. A lot of nights, Finn just watched Travis with a creased brow.

Nearly two weeks after Mike brought Angel his long-awaited letter, Finn asked Angel at bedtime, "Why can't Uncle Trav go back to living with Mike? Mike's nice. Mike knows how to live with Uncle Trav."

"Mike made a mistake, and Uncle Trav isn't sure he wants to forgive him."

"What did Mike do?"

"He kept something a secret because he was mad at me and thought he was protecting Ryan."

Finn thought for a minute, climbed out of bed, and then ran into the living room where, today, Travis was wallowing on the couch. Finn hopped up onto the couch and wrapped his arms around Travis' neck. He hugged Travis and then studied him. Travis shied away under the scrutiny. Angel would be the first to admit that a stare from Finn made him uncomfortable. It was easy to forget he was only six under that stare.

Finally, Finn said, "You shouldn't be mad at Mike. He was just trying to be a good friend."

Travis tilted his head and ruffled Finn's thick hair. "You're very smart for a six-year-old."

"Grammy always says that when we talk on the phone."

"You must not get it from your dad," Travis said and Angel snorted.

"Finn, you really need to go to bed," Angel said. "You have school tomorrow."

Finn sighed, but bounced off the couch.

"Goodnight, Finn," Travis called. "See you tomorrow."

"I hope not," Finn responded. Angel laughed with his whole body at the insulted look on Travis' face.

"I think he just means that he hopes you go home," Angel appeased.

"Don't try to stick up for your insolent spawn," Travis muttered.

Angel chuckled and went to tuck Finn in. Finn looked apprehensive when Angel walked into the room. "You don't think Uncle Trav is mad, do you?"

"No, I think you just gave him the kick in the butt he needs."

Finn's face turned into a grin, and he looked satisfied enough to go to sleep.

"Goodnight, Finn."

Angel wandered back into the living room to find Travis still sitting on the couch. Now, though, Travis was staring at his phone with a concerted look.

"You should call him," Angel said finally.

"He made you miserable for months."

"Not really. I made myself miserable."

"He compounded it."

"That may be true, but he did it to protect Ryan. Would you have given Ryan a heart-bearing letter from me if you knew he had cheated on me?"

"Absolutely not."

Angel raised his eyebrows and Travis huffed.

"That's totally different."

"Is it?"

Travis sighed. "All right."

"Travis, you know I'm really grateful that you're so angry on my behalf, but even you were saying I was being a prick about the entire situation. I did some really shitty things, and I don't really blame Mike for what he did. If I can forgive him, so should you."

"I just never imagined that Mike could be so vindictive."

"I don't know. Maybe it was just protectiveness."

"Stop sticking up for him," Travis groused.

"I'm just trying to be less of a dick and start being Reasonable Angel again."

Travis laughed. "That would be nice; I'm not very good at being the reasonable one."

"I know."

"It's very strenuous."

Angel dropped onto the couch next to Travis, burying his face in Travis' neck. Travis pressed his cheek to Angel's hair.

"So you think I should call him?" Travis mumbled.

"Yeah, I do."

"Can I invite him over here? I feel like if I go back to our... his place, we'll just end up in bed together."

"Sure."

Travis sighed, but scrolled through his contacts anyway. The conversation that followed was stilted, but Travis' smile told Angel he'd probably be out of the apartment soon.

"He said he'll be over after his shift."

"Superhero movies?"

"Superhero movies," Travis agreed.

Angel went into the kitchen, grabbed a two-liter bottle of soda, and popped some buttery popcorn. Travis had already set up the DVD player. He fell asleep halfway through the first movie with his head in Angel's lap. Angel knew he should probably sleep too, but he was actually a little nervous about this reunion. It felt like precursor for his reunion with Ryan. He wanted it to turn out well.

There was a gentle knock on the door as Angel nodded off. He extricated himself from Travis' firm grip and, when he opened the door, Mike was there, shifting back and forth on his long legs. He looked incredibly young and Angel, for a second, had the urge to protect him.

"Hi," Angel said.

"I'm sorry," Mike said. "Really, man, I'm very sorry."

"It's okay, I promise. Go win him back."

Angel was always alarmed by how endearing Mike's smile was. Wanting to protect Mike was like pure instinct, like protecting Finn or Rosa. Angel patted Mike's shoulder as he passed him into the apartment.

Travis' arms were crossed, but Angel could see the hope in his sleep-blurred eyes. Travis and Mike stood for a moment, just looking at each other. Mike kept scuffing his feet and looking down. Angel went into the kitchen to make tea, something his mom would do if people were having a serious conversation.

When he walked back into the living room, Mike was sitting on the couch looking down at his twiddling thumbs and Travis was in the chair, talking in low tones. Travis paused momentarily in his speech when he saw Angel. All three sets of lips turned up tentatively, Angel handed them both mugs, and then headed down the hallway to his room. He vaguely registered Travis climbing into his bed in the wee hours of the morning.

"Everything okay?" Angel croaked.

"Yeah, thanks, Angel."

Later, Angel woke to the smell of breakfast cooking. He could feel the grin spread across his face. He shoved Travis' shoulder, eliciting a grumble before he smelled it too.

"Part of the reason I wanted Mike back," he joked, and Angel laughed.

As much as Angel would've liked to stay in bed all day, he needed to wake up Finn and get him ready for school.

Finn skidded into the kitchen and ran to find Travis.

"Hi, Mike," Finn said, very emphatically.

"Hey," Mike responded as he flipped a pancake, "Want some pancakes?"

"Yeah!"

Travis kissed the back of Mike's neck, and Angel was expecting a heavy sigh from Finn. Instead, his son grinned and clapped lightly. He ruffled Finn's hair.

***

The first thing Ryan's brain registered was that his leg felt like a smoldering fire. It was hot and achy, but the burning sensation was muted. The rest of his body felt heavy and uncontrollable, and his thoughts were jumbled, fuzzy, and nearly incoherent. He blinked awake and the sterilized hospital room, although he should have expected it, was still shocking.

He pressed the red call button by his bed. A middle-aged woman rushed in, smiling reassuringly at him when she saw his confused expression.

"It's good to see you awake, Sergeant Garry."

"Ryan," he corrected weakly. "What happened— where am I? What's wrong with my leg?"

"You drove off the road when you saw a suicide bomber, and you saved everyone in your caravan. But your Humvee wasn't far enough away when the bomb went off, and it flipped. You're in Germany. You shattered your femur; it'll need surgery. Right now, it's bandaged up pretty well, but the surgery will be necessary before it starts to completely heal itself."

"Has somebody called my parents?"

"Yes; they're flying to New York to be there when you get there. The recommendation is, since you're relatively stable, that you're flown to a New York hospital to have your surgery and recover there. This surgery is completely routine, but you would have to be here for two more weeks if we did it here. We speculated that you'd rather be near home."

Ryan furrowed his brow. "How long is recovery going to take?"

"At least six months. Shattering your femur is serious. It's a long process."

"So I can make it back to America without a problem?"

"Most likely."

"I'd like to go as soon as possible."

"I thought you'd say that; there's a flight back tomorrow morning."

Ryan called his parents, who both sobbed in relief when he told them his leg hurt, but he was fine. They had a hotel room at the place they used to stay at when they would visit him at West Point. He couldn't deny that he was glad to go home alive, but he did feel guilty for leaving his comrades, his friends, in the dangerous situation they were supposed to be in together.

The transport was painful and exhausting, but seeing his parents when he landed made it worth it. He let his mom baby him, and she left him with a box of her homemade cookies and a hand-knitted sweater. He cuddled down into the sweater and begged for milk from the nurse to eat half a dozen cookies with.

The doctors met with him the morning after he arrived and explained the surgery planned for that afternoon. It was all big words and medical jargon. All Ryan could think about was how close he was to Angel, how much he wanted to see him, how much he wanted those lips to kiss him. Yearning was bad enough; having to do it alone was worse.

He didn't get the chance to call Angel until two days after his surgery, when his mom had her phone fully charged and left it with him while she grabbed dinner. He hoped Angel would pick up to an unfamiliar number. The phone rang five times and Ryan almost gave up.

"Hello?" Angel said tentatively.

"Hey," Ryan said. "It's Ryan."

"Fuck," Angel sighed, but happily— or at least, Ryan hoped so. "Where are you?"

"NY State Army Hospital," Ryan said, and then, quickly, "I'm okay."

"You wouldn't be at a hospital in America if you were okay," Angel said.

"Okay, I broke my femur, but they've completed the surgery. They said the healing is going really well."

"Good," Angel commented.

"You sound far off," Ryan said. He hoped it didn't sound as desperate as he felt.

"I was just looking up how far away you are."

"You can't come."

"Why not?"

Ryan sighed. He would have liked nothing more than to see Angel; he'd never hated the rules more. But they were still the rules. "Because I won't be able to hide how I feel about you."

"I'll figure something out."

"You will?"

"Yeah, I need to see you, make sure you're okay, see you for myself," Angel confessed. "Plus, Finn will really want to see you. He's missed you and your letters."

"I'm sorry about that."

"Don't be, especially now that you're so close. Just say we can come."

Ryan felt himself smile. "You can come."

"We'll be there Saturday, bright and early at ten."

"I can't wait."

"Me neither."

It was hard to convince his parents to take in the sights on Saturday morning. There was nothing they hadn't seen before, but they agreed, thinking he needed a break from them. He felt guilty for making them feel overbearing, but they read him so well, and he didn't want them there while he mooned over Angel.

He woke up early on Saturday, feeling like he was getting ready for a first date. His hair was getting a little long. He hadn't gotten it cut since he was near an actual base overseas. It was soft when he ran his hands through it, hoping it looked okay.

There was a soft knock on his door, and then Finn was sprinting into the room, babbling and jumping next to his bed. Ryan reached out to ruffle the boy's dark locks. Then Angel walked in slowly; Mike was right behind him, and Ryan realized in confusion that their hands were linked. Mike turned to shut the door, and Angel immediately dropped his hand. Ryan's face must have shown his confusion and discomfort.

"It's to throw off the nurses," Angel explained. "I was worried my fondness for you might show through, and I know how much the military means to you." A smile. "Who knows why."

Ryan ignored the second comment, because Angel was striding over to kiss him, and he didn't want to bicker today. The kiss was gentle, and Ryan wondered if they could fall right back into what they had before he left. He didn't see the shimmer of guilt in Angel's eyes when he pulled back, too distracted by Finn trying to get his attention.

Chapter Eight

Angel wasn't sure how to feel now that Ryan was back. Relieved, for sure, but the guilt had also intensified. It was easier to brush off the one-night stands when he thought Ryan had stopped caring. Now that he was back and Angel realized he never stopped caring, Angel felt his wrongdoings pressing on his conscience. The only thing saving him was that Ryan had told him not to wait for him. Ryan had made him promise not to resent him, and Angel didn't; he resented himself. It was a misunderstanding beyond their control.

They visited Ryan again, and Finn brought his art supplies. While Ryan didn't have many artistic skills, he spent much of their visit with Finn pushed against his side, shading a tree, and laughing as Finn told him about school. Angel wished their lives could be easier. Not that gay relationships were unanimously accepted, but they were relatively so in mainstream culture, especially in New York City. The military was stopping them.

They were on the phone one night after their visit when Angel finally confronted the topic.

"No one would blame you if you left now," Angel said.

"I don't know about that. Have you met Pete?" Ryan's voice was teasing, but it had an undercurrent of non-discussion.

" 'Don't ask, don't tell' could run our relationship into the ground."

"We don't have to let it. The military means a lot to me. It's part of who I am. Leaving will run us into the ground. This isn't up for discussion."

"Ryan," Angel sighed, letting the word hang before asking, "When are you going to get out of the hospital?"

"A few days, but they say I have to rest, not walk much for another week or so. My mom wants to come home with me, but we're not sure how that's going to work out. She's got a job back in Iowa."

"You could come stay with me and Finn."

"Angel?"

Angel barrelled on. "Give us those two months before you're supposed to start desk duty, and then you can make the decision about whether you're going to go back."

"I'll go back, Angel. That's not really up for debate."

"The offer still stands."

"I voted for Obama; he says he wants to repeal 'Don't ask, don't tell.' "

"I voted for him too," Angel said flatly. Political promises didn't always mean much.

"I don't want to hide away, Angel. I need you to know that."

"It's hard to feel like that when we have to sneak around."

Ryan sighed. "So you can't come to my place—trust me, not a big loss; you can't meet my work friends, also not a big loss. This is in your head, Angel."

"Two months?" Angel pushed.

"Fine, two months."

Angel's flash of anger made the guilt subside a little. He tried to rationalize his actions. After all, he didn't actually cheat, because Ryan had given him permission. It sounded weak to his own ears.

Travis kept telling him that he should tell Ryan anyway; Mike kept saying he should get tested. Angel wasn't sure he liked Mike all that much anymore. He was sure that guy had put on a condom. He wasn't a complete idiot, after all.

***

Ryan wasn't sure how to convince his mom to go back to Iowa, but he absolutely had to. Angel had offered to let him stay at his place, even though it did come with the added pressure of Angel wanting him to end his career. Since he now had a two-month leave of absence before he even had to go back to desk duty, he was going to take full advantage of Angel's offer. It was selfish, he knew, because he had no intention of quitting, but he wanted what he could get from Angel. Yet, his mother wouldn't listen to his reassurances that he'd be fine on his own. She wouldn't even listen to reason; he kept reminding her that she'd probably lose her job at the library if she didn't go home soon. She acted like he was a ghost come back to life, and she couldn't let him slip through her fingers. He knew his parents weren't strapped for cash, but they weren't made of money either. They both needed to work for their lives to be comfortable.

"A friend says I can stay with him while I get better."

"I want to meet him."

"Mom," Ryan whined, like a twelve-year-old.

"If he's going to be taking care of my baby, I need to meet him."

Ryan was panicking; he could feel his heart racing and the hairs standing up on the back of his neck. He wanted to run, but his mind couldn't come up with an excuse, so he just nodded and mumbled, "Okay."

He felt bad asking Angel to come up during the week, but Angel didn't make a peep about it. In fact, he seemed to think it completely reasonable for Ryan's mom to want to meet him.

Angel and Finn arrived first. Finn was showing Ryan books he got at the school library and explaining how he was going to Chicago to visit his Grammy and Poppa for Christmas break. Angel had his hand on Ryan's thigh, leaning back in the stiff visitor's chair. His face was soft, and Ryan was pretty sure he'd fallen asleep with his head resting against the wall. Ryan should've probably moved Angel's hand, but the nurses always knocked, and his mom wasn't expected for another hour. The warmth and intimacy that radiated up his leg was making him take more risks than he should. Ryan was so entranced with Finn's dramatic recount of his trip to see the Nutcracker with Travis that he didn't hear the door open or the light tap of his mom's shoes when she arrived fifteen minutes early.

"Oh," she gasped, and Ryan's first inclination was to push Angel's hand off his thigh. He wanted to brush it off, and she would probably accept that. She would never mention it again, but she would wonder. He looked down at the hand and then into his mom's eyes and back again to the paint-stained hand. Then, he reached down and threaded his fingers through Angel's. Angel mumbled a little, squeezing his hand.

Ryan couldn't read his mother's face. The fear that she would reject this, reject him, terrified him. Finn, sensing the uncertainty, stopped talking and crammed his face into Ryan's neck.

"It's okay, bud, that's my mom," Ryan whispered into Finn's hair.

"Ryan," she asked tentatively, "Who's this?"

"This is Finn," he said, running his other hand through Finn's hair, and then he lifted his and Angel's clasped hands. "And this is Angel."

"I know who Angel Posadas is, darling. Hello, Finn," she said, and it was tentative but still warm, still his mom. He felt tears prickle his eyes and went to rub them, the motion of the gesture jolting Angel awake. At first, he stretched slowly, but then his eyes landed on Ryan's mother and he all but jumped from his chair.

"Hello, Mrs. Garry, it's wonderful to meet you," Angel croaked, blinking his eyes furiously.

"Hello, it's lovely to meet you too. I love your work." She paused, tilting her head, and asked curiously, "Why were you and my son holding hands?"

Ryan knew that she knew the answer. She was offering them a way out. If they weren't ready, she'd be okay with that. She wouldn't force them out of the closet; she'd leave this moment right here.

Ryan could see Angel trying to formulate a response, and he felt something click in his chest. He loved Angel; Angel who didn't want to hide, but would do it for Ryan. Angel, for whom this was familiar and yet brand new, who had put up with Ryan's insecurities and hesitancy.

"We're together," Ryan said definitively. Angel snapped his head to stare at Ryan; Ryan sent him what he hoped was a reassuring look through his terror. Ryan reached his hand out again, and Angel's fingers wove with his.

"Okay," she said softly, "So this is who's going to take care of you?"

"Yeah," Ryan confirmed, and she nodded her head. Angel squeezed his hand and he returned the gesture.

"Clearly, I was worried about nothing."

Ryan let out a choked laugh, and Angel leaned down to kiss Ryan's head. Finn unfurled himself and glanced between the adults.

"Are you going to be my new grandma?" Finn asked tentatively.

"Finn Posadas," Angel hissed, but Ryan's mom just laughed.

"Maybe someday," she said. Finn smiled; Ryan couldn't look at Angel's reaction.

Ryan's mom only stayed to get him settled in Angel's apartment. He asked her not to tell his dad and she said she'd try, but she was almost giddy that he was with Angel, of all people, and Ryan knew not to take it as a promise.

Ryan hadn't lived with anyone since he was at West Point. He thought it might be difficult or annoying, but Angel and Finn were really very easy to live with. It was almost as quiet as living by himself. Angel and Finn were happy to go about their lives at a library level volume.

Mrs. Hardy dropped Finn off after school every day, and Ryan liked the company. He made Finn a snack and then they did his homework together while Angel was in the studio. He got to know Finn very well.

When winter break came closer, Finn got more excited to go visit his mom's family, and Ryan got sadder. This wasn't just playing nice with his boyfriend's son; it was starting to feel like they had their own parent-child relationship. Finn wanted him to do bedtime as often as he wanted Angel to.

While his relationship with Finn was moving forward, though, his relationship with Angel seemed to be moving in the opposite direction.
***

There was a horrible part of Angel that wished this wasn't working out as well as it was. He wished he could cut ties with Ryan and never tell him about his indiscretions, on account of him and Finn not getting along. Of course, what was happening was the

119

opposite: Finn and Ryan were getting so close that a weaker man would worry about being phased out.

He knew Ryan was beginning to wonder why he was so distant. Ryan had recovered enough now for sex, but that would mean Angel would have to explain... things. He hadn't gotten the results back from the tests he took nearly a week ago. He wouldn't subject Ryan to that; he cared too much to risk him getting infected.

After he'd put Finn to bed, Angel walked back into the living room where Ryan was resting on the couch, watching football. When he got close, Ryan grabbed his hand and tugged him toward the couch.

"Come on, Angel," Ryan whispered.

Angel felt a tug in his navel that overrode the twinge in his mind. He gave into the puppy-dog eyes and straddled Ryan, trying to avoid putting any weight on the injured leg. Angel cradled Ryan's head and kissed him, feeling Ryan moan into the kiss and move his hand to Angel's hips. Angel had missed this, the intimate contact. Sexual contact was one thing, but this devotion and the seeds of love were what separated interactions with Ryan from everybody else. Angel was quickly so lost in the slide of their tongues that he didn't notice Ryan's hands slipping into his boxer-briefs until Ryan was squeezing, his fingers drifting towards Angel's cleft. Angel hoped Ryan couldn't taste the bile that rose in the back of his throat.

"Ryan, we can't," Angel whispered into Ryan's mouth.

"I know it will be annoying with my leg, but if you ride me, we should be fine, right?" He suddenly looked incredibly young, and Angel wanted to shield Ryan from what he had to say.

Angel pulled away and leaned back, still sure to keep the weight off Ryan's healing femur. "I got tested Wednesday. I don't want to risk anything until I get the results."

The confusion on Ryan's face made Angel hate himself that little bit more. "I cheated, Ryan."

"No, you didn't," Ryan said slowly. "I told you to go out with other people. I just never thought you would."

"That's not fair, Ryan."

"I know," Ryan said, and he kissed Angel with remorse. "Tell me what happened."

"That's not necessary."

"Yes, it is."

And so, Angel explained his recklessness, and every word was excruciating.

***

At first, the news left Ryan feeling sad and betrayed, but then he found himself angry. He knew he shouldn't be; he knew he promised he wouldn't be, but he was. He brushed past Angel at every turn. He could barely be civil, and he didn't want to be. He slept on Finn's trundle bed, even though it was low and difficult for him to get on. It made his leg ache, but sleeping on the trundle bed was better than digging his face into Angel's shoulder blades and forgiving him while begging for forgiveness of his own.

They skittered around each other, and Ryan was somewhat ashamed to admit that he muttered insults under his breath when he got too close. It got worse when Finn's aunt whisked him off to Chicago for break— until Angel came home from work on Wednesday, smiling.

"The test came back negative," Angel breathed. Ryan abruptly wanted to smack the smile off him.

"You think that's the only part that matters?"

"No, but…" Angel trailed off at the look on Ryan's face.

"Maybe now, I can show you why having sex with other people was such a bad idea," Ryan hissed, and a shocked look crossed Angel's face.

"They'll never be able to make you feel what I can," Ryan said, shoving Angel towards the bedroom.

Angel snorted derisively. "They were both more experienced than you."

"Shut up," Ryan said, pushing Angel against the wall. He felt set alight, his body on autopilot. He bit at Angel's lip and palmed him through his pants until Angel bucked into his hand and Ryan snorted, pulling away and dragging him toward the bedroom. He propped himself on the end of the bed with his good leg and tugged Angel towards him, pushing up his shirt without preamble and mouthing at his stomach.

"Take it off," Ryan ordered, as he got to work on Angel's pants and underwear.

"Back up," Angel said, pushing Ryan backwards. Ryan dragged himself up until his back was pressed against the headboard. Angel loomed above him, his dick right in Ryan's face, and Ryan's mouth flooded with saliva. He wasted no time licking up the underside, engulfing Angel entirely in his mouth. Expert or not, Angel bucked forward, his fingers wrapping around the base of his cock as if to stay his orgasm. Ryan let Angel fuck his mouth, but he also let his teeth catch at the skin as he sucked, taking a bitter pleasure in Angel's soft, pained sounds. Angel didn't stop, though, and soon enough, Ryan had him by the hips, guiding the motion. It was too deep now, Ryan's eyes burning, but his own cock was thickening in his pants, and when he swallowed around the head of Angel's dick, that was it; Angel came so deep in Ryan's throat, he couldn't even taste it.

When he pulled off at last, Angel slumped down against him, and Ryan asked, "Was she as good?"

"You know she wasn't," Angel said, pressing their foreheads together. His movements were sleepy and sated, but Ryan was far from done.

"I'm going to fuck you better than that guy ever thought of," Ryan growled. "Flip over onto your knees."

"Don't be an idiot," Angel whispered against Ryan's neck.

"I want to fuck you."

"And you can do that, sitting just like that."

Ryan huffed out a breath. "But it won't be the same. You'll be in control."

"I'm not letting you fuck up your leg because I let some bear fuck me when I was drunk. That's stupid, Ryan. You'll always be better."

Ryan furrowed his brow. "That's not what you said before."

"You never let me clarify. I just said they were more experienced, but Ryan— everything has always been better with you."

Angel pushed Ryan's sweatpants and underwear down over the head of his cock, his hands gentle now, and Ryan breathed out, let himself shift the mood. They prepped Angel together, rolled a condom down Ryan's straining cock, and then Angel was guiding him in, his face tight with the burn he felt. At first, Angel didn't move, and Ryan let him adjust, although his hips were begging to buck up into the tightness. When Angel relaxed, though, it was with a nod and a sigh, and Ryan's gut flooded with heat, realizing Angel was letting Ryan guide their movements, even like this, letting Ryan rock them toward oblivion.

Chapter Nine

The weekend Finn was gone, Mike and Travis invited them to spend a few days in their guest bedroom. It was small, but Angel and Ryan weren't all that picky. They went out to dinner at Mike's restaurant while he was working and let him choose their courses. Then, they made the obligatory trip to Travis' show, now the eighth time Angel had seen it since its debut. Travis dragged them to some club having a Christmas party, and Angel tried to keep up with the cocktails Travis was drinking like orange juice. Mike and Ryan stuck to the seasonal beer that tasted distinctly like gingerbread.

Angel was drunk enough to enjoy the way Ryan tugged him in between his legs and pressed his fingers into Angel's hips. Angel knew Ryan desperately wanted to dance, but was glued to the barstool because of his leg. Angel spent most of his time figuring out ways to turn Ryan on, which wasn't difficult at all given their close proximity, but Angel was never aware of how effective skimming touches were on his boyfriend. Like how dragging his nail across the peek-a-boo of skin at his hip caused his dick to jump more than the downright grope that the front of his pants received. Even though Ryan seemed to be trying to keep some kind of decorum, Angel was having no part of it. When he sloppily kissed Ryan, his tongue stroked against Ryan's, and he pulled back abruptly.

"Did you eat the gingerbread man?"

"Angel?" Ryan asked, his fingers playing with the hem of Angel's sweater as Angel struggled to focus on Ryan's face.

"You taste like the gingerbread man."

"I drank a beer that tastes like gingerbread."

"Right, did you know I like gingerbread?"

"Did you know you're drunk?"

"Am not."

"Are too."

"Shut up, you don't know anything," Angel pouted. "I liked it better when you were quiet and we were kissing."

"Me too," Ryan said affectionately, kissing Angel's nose.

"Not exactly what I was going for."

Angel dragged Ryan off the barstool and maneuvered them so Ryan's back was pressed against a wall in a dimly-lit corner. Angel was careful not to put pressure on the full-leg brace or knock the crutch tucked under Ryan's arm, but he managed to press himself flush to Ryan despite the obstacles. He mouthed at Ryan's neck, blood rising under his lips, and Angel knew there'd be a mark there tomorrow. He would never admit to how much that thrilled him. He wouldn't admit that he constantly wanted to leave little possessive symbols all over Ryan's body.

His dick pressed painfully against his zipper, and he pushed his pelvis against Ryan, watching the pleasurable sensations play out on Ryan's features. On the one hand, he knew this was turning Ryan on, if his hard dick and breathy moans were to be trusted, but he also knew that Ryan was far from an exhibitionist. Another slow undulation of his pelvis, and Angel could see the inhibitions dissolving under a haze of want.

"Now, now, now, let's not make Ryan cum in his pants in the middle of the club, Mr. Exhibitionist."

Travis' voice made them both jump apart. Angel growled at Travis and Ryan sagged in relief, adjusting himself so his hardness wasn't as obvious. Angel wondered again why he and Travis were friends.

"Fuck you."

"That's Mike's job."

"Come on, gentlemen, no fighting," Mike warned, running a hand through his hair as he threw his other arm around Travis' shoulders. "The night is young."

***

"Young" was pushing it, but they decided to walk the two short blocks back to Travis and Mike's place. Ryan was trying to avoid the icy patches while simultaneously making sure Angel didn't drunkenly stumble into a snowbank.

"Abstentious," Angel said suddenly: "given to or marked by restraint in the satisfaction of one's appetites."

"What are you doing?" Ryan asked curiously, a smile creeping onto his face despite the cold air that nipped at his cheeks and the pain throbbing in his leg.

"Proving that I'm not drunk," Angel reported matter-of-factly.   "A-B-S-T-E-N-T-I-O-U-S. Abstentious. People who are abstentious are usually pretentious and boring."

"Okay," Ryan said.

"Diffident: shy, quiet, or modest. D-I-F-F-I-D-E-N-T. Diffident. My son inherited his diffident behavior from me; his mother was quite gregarious."

"What is he doing?" Travis demanded.

"Proving he's not drunk."

"By spelling?"

"Yep."

Travis laughed. "Spell supercalifragilisticexpialidocious."

Angel huffed. "That's an easy one. Supercalifragilisticexpialidocious: extraordinarily good, wonderful. S-U-P-E-R-C-A-L-F-R-A-G-I-L-I-S-T-I-C-E-X-P-I-A-L-D-O-C-I-O-U-S. Supercalifragilisticexpialidocious. It is supercalifragilisticexpialidocious to be with you all tonight."

Ryan and Mike looked at Angel as if he'd sprouted two heads and started chanting to Satan in Latin, while Travis just laughed hysterically. "It's a party trick," he explained. "I don't know why that's always the word people make someone spell, but he started doing this in college and it's fucking hilarious to watch people hear him do it for the first time. He won some spelling bee when he was a kid and people always said, "But I bet you can't spell supercalifragilisticexpialidocious." So he memorized it, and now, I make him spell it whenever he's drunk. It's won us a lot of bets."

As they walked into the lobby, Ryan heard the soft undertone of Angel's voice and asked, "Are you still spelling?"

"Maybe," Angel said sulkily. "I'm not drunk."

Ryan chuckled and kissed Angel's forehead as they waited for the elevator. He slid an arm around Angel's waist and Angel made a contented noise, placing a hand on Ryan's stomach. They stumbled into the elevator when it arrived, and Ryan was a little worried he might get to see more of Mike than desired when Travis' hand slid into Mike's trench coat. Thankfully, Travis dragged Mike off down the hallway quicker than Ryan could manage with his leg and Angel, who seemed half-asleep.

The second Ryan got them across the threshold, Travis slammed and locked the door. Mike called out, "Goodnight," as Travis hauled him wordlessly into the bedroom. In their own little room, Angel fell heavily onto the bed and immediately wiggled out of everything but his boxers. Ryan was slower, but after a few aching minutes, he managed to shed most of his clothing.

"I wanna blow you," Angel murmured when Ryan tried to arrange himself into a position he could sleep in.

"You don't have to," Ryan responded, even though his dick was still half-hard from the club.

"But I want to."

Ryan couldn't disagree with that, so he watched as Angel crawled down the bed. Angel tugged down Ryan's underwear, and Ryan felt himself twitch as

Angel traced a line up the underside of his cock and then breathed hotly over the damp skin. Ryan leaned his head back and relaxed into the mattress, feeling Angel suck a bruise into his good thigh and then kiss the spot gently. The contrast of pain and tenderness made pre-cum leak onto Ryan's navel. Then the kissing stopped, and at first, Ryan thought he was being teased, but there was still a heavy weight on his thigh. He looked down and Angel's eyes were closed. Ryan bit his lip and groaned, gently pushing at Angel's shoulder, turning him on his back.

"Angel," he called, shaking Angel's shoulder. "Come on, I can't pull you up the bed on my own." His tone was amused, but leaning into exasperation. Ryan hooked his hands under his arms and pulled. Angel made an uncomfortable noise, but moved with Ryan's tugs. As Ryan arranged them on the bed so that Angel was pressed against Ryan's side, Angel groggily mumbled into Ryan's collarbone, "Love you."

"I think I love you too," Ryan responded, with his heart pounding in his chest. He was nervous about these words, not that Angel was going to remember them at all. It was the first time either had uttered them. Even if it didn't count, maybe it was practice for the sober repeat performance.

Ryan woke up early, as he usually did on weekends. He turned on the big-screen TV and flipped naturally to the Sunday morning cartoons he usually watched with Finn. It was an hour before anybody else woke up: just Mike, wrapped in a duvet. He chugged a cup of coffee and then started on breakfast, leaving the blanket. Ryan offered to help and Mike smiled blearily at him, shaking his head no. As usual, the smell of food drew Angel out of the bedroom.

"I'm not sure if I'm going to be able to eat," Angel announced, sitting gently next to Ryan and burying his face into Ryan's neck. Ryan snorted and rubbed Angel's back cautiously.

"You know you don't have to watch cartoons when Finn isn't here, right?" Angel asked into Ryan's neck.

"I've just been using Finn as an excuse."

Angel snorted, and Ryan added, "I miss him."

He could feel Angel's smile in his neck, and he hoped Angel knew how sincere that statement was. "Me too."

"How many more days?"

"Only four."

"Four is so many," Ryan whined.

"We'll Skype with him tonight."

They ate breakfast; Ryan dug right into the biscuits and gravy, while Angel only munched slowly on a biscuit. Travis and Mike had to leave early, and Angel and Ryan spent the rest of the day running errands around the city and looking at the Christmas lights. They went to the art gallery, and Ryan was amazed by the beautiful display of Angel's work. Paul let him know what had been sold, and what he'd like to see by Angel's next deadline.

"When do you usually paint?" Ryan asked curiously. He'd never seen Angel paint. A lot of his day-to-day work seemed to involve managing the business side of things.

"Sometimes, when you and Finn are asleep, I'll stay up and paint. I used to paint in the studio in the back at the gallery every Sunday while Finn hung out with Rosa, but I haven't done that in a while."

"Why not?"

"Because I haven't," Angel shrugged.

"You don't have to stop painting for me."

"I'm not; I just don't usually want to leave home anymore, and Rosa has been busy with finals and her new boyfriend."

"Well, I could watch Finn from now on so you can paint. We could make a day of it."

"That would be nice."

Ryan nodded and Angel smiled like Ryan just offered him the world. Ryan's breath hitched when he realized that he'd have to go back to work soon. He couldn't stay in this domestic bliss forever, and Angel wouldn't always smile at him like that. In Ryan's real world, guys didn't just play house with guys.

In the afternoon, they called Finn before ordering take-out from the place Mike recommended, and watched movies on Travis' ostentatious TV. Ryan loved how Angel got so cuddly when he was hungover and relaxed. They kissed, but without expectations. They went to bed before either Travis or Mike came back from work and made love slowly, carefully, as if they had forever to themselves.

The next morning, Angel made French toast for breakfast in thanks to Travis and Mike for letting them stay. Then it was time to help them set up for the Christmas party they'd planned for that night.

Ryan got ready last because it would take him the longest just to shower, and he didn't want anyone to be waiting for him to finish with the bathroom. When he went back into the bedroom they'd been sharing, Angel was wearing the extra flannel shirt Ryan brought, which didn't compensate for the socks he forgot. The sight of Angel in his clothes sparked a rush of possessiveness in Ryan that made him want to throw Angel ass-up over the mattress.

"Holy fuck," Ryan growled. Angel raised his eyebrows and winked.

"Thanks for packing an extra shirt."

"Anything for you, babe."

As much as Ryan's dick disapproved, people started arriving, and Angel and Ryan were pulled in opposite directions. Mike demanded Angel help him set out more appetizers, and Travis dragged Ryan to the bar.

"Your boyfriend has horrible taste in alcohol, and I figure you're military, so you're probably good at following directions. So I am going to teach you how to make my signature drinks for tonight, and you're going to help get them out. Got it?"

Ryan nodded and listened closely as Travis taught him how to make the "Santa Baby" and the "Grinch." Ryan handed out about fifteen of each drink before Travis dismissed him to go find Angel.

He found Angel in deep conversation with a man wearing a sport jacket and a Rolex. The man was looking at Angel hungrily, and Ryan felt his stomach acid rise into his mouth. He knew it was posturing, but Angel was *his,* and he unbuttoned his shirt so the mark Angel sucked into his throat the other night was obvious. He leaned his crutch against the wall that led to the bedroom, out of the line of vision of this douche. He limped over to Angel and had to press his lips together to keep from yelping in pain. But dammit, it was worth it. He put his arm around Angel's shoulders and kissed his cheek.

"Hey, babe," Ryan said.

"Hi," Angel said, amusement playing over his features. He turned to the man he was talking to and made introductions. "This is Ryan. Ryan, this is Ron, he's a friend of Travis'."

"Hello," the man said stiffly.

"Hello," Ryan smirked.

Angel continued his conversation and Ryan felt, despite himself, slightly ignored and insecure. They were talking about an art movement Ryan didn't understand well, and he was swiftly losing any assuredness he had about their relationship, which he recognized was dumb. He ran his hand up and down Angel's back, and Angel kept glancing at him questioningly. Ryan was about to lean over and kiss Angel again when Angel ended the conversation.

"It was nice talking to you, but I'm famished. We need to go find some food." He smiled at Ron and then all but dragged Ryan away. Ryan could barely keep up without his crutch.

"What the hell?" Angel demanded, once he'd found them somewhere secluded enough.

"What?"

"You don't usually go caveman on me."

"I wasn't…" Ryan trailed off when Angel gave him a skeptical look. "He looked like he wanted to push you to your knees and make you suck him off," Ryan hissed, and Angel shook his head in irritation. "Plus, it was clear he had money."

"What does that have to do with anything?"

"He could provide better for you and Finn than I could ever think of," Ryan said, looking down at his feet. He looked up quickly when Angel hit him hard.

"I'm not some damsel in distress, you fuck. Was this what you were like when you were playing straight? Because I'm telling you, girls don't like that shit, either. Plus, the minute that guy heard about Finn, he would go running for the hills."

"That's not true; Finn is great."

"God, you're so fucking adorable," Angel said after a second's hesitation, surging up and kissing him fiercely. Pulling away for breath, he added, "I hate to admit that I almost popped a boner from your jealousy. Ugh."

"Fuck," Ryan whined and leaned in to kiss him more. He forgot about his leg and went to push Angel against the wall of their nook; the sudden rush of pain was enough to remind him. He doubled over with the shock of it, sucking in deep breaths.

"You stupid, jealous moron," Angel said, moving him carefully into the nearest chair. He searched about for the crutch, spotted it, and laid it down across Ryan's lap with a pointed look. "You know what I said Saturday night when we were falling asleep... I meant it."

Ryan startled. "I thought you hadn't remembered."

"No, I remember, and I meant it, Ryan. I think I'm falling in love with you. So you don't have to worry about some self-centered old guy. I don't want anyone else."

Ryan's mouth felt dry. "Same."

"Come on, I just laid it out there in front of you. The least you could do is say it too."

The words seemed to spill out in slow motion. Ryan felt like an actor in the film of his own life. "I have no doubt I'm falling in love with you."

"Had to show me up, didn't you?" Angel huffed, and Ryan smiled at him, pulling him down for a kiss. Angel pulled away and reprimanded him. "Now, keep your crutch with you and use it. You don't want to make your leg worse."

"Okay," Ryan agreed, and followed him back to the party.

Chapter Ten

Angel's mom had always insisted on celebrating Christmas in a big way, as a time for family to be together. There'd never been a church connection for them, but the food and love and gifts more than filled up that hole. She had been brought up religious, but grown agnostic in adulthood, and now liked to celebrate holidays just because they brought families closer together rather than for their religious purposes. This year, Angel, more than ever, understood that notion, which was weird, because his closest family member was eight hundred miles away in Chicago with his cousins. Celebrating Christmas with Ryan was one of the most exhilarating and perplexing things Angel had ever experienced. He was more exuberant than Finn, talking a mile a minute, hands going all over the place. Angel could feel the fondness and second-hand embarrassment bloom in his chest because really, no adult should be that excited ever, unless they'd just won a million dollars or something; yet, it was still entertaining, and somehow so very typically Ryan.

Ryan woke Angel up with breakfast in bed on Christmas morning: gingerbread-men-shaped pancakes with hints of molasses, ginger, cloves, and cinnamon. He tried to keep Ryan in bed with sticky kisses and promises of blowjobs, but Ryan dragged him out of bed to open presents. There wasn't much to open under the tree since they'd promised most of it for when Finn got home, but they exchanged gifts with each other. Angel wasn't sure what to buy Ryan, especially when Ryan was tight-lipped about anything he wanted, so he went for a set of vintage comics. Ryan received his gifts with reverent awe, which made Angel feel inexplicably bashful.

He wasn't sure what he was expecting from Ryan, but it wasn't what he got. He opened up a case of his favorite paints and a plethora of new brushes. Ryan looked up at him hesitantly and explained that he called Paul to find out his favorite brand. Angel bit his lip and decided to convince Ryan there and then that now would be a good time for that Christmas blowjob, right there on the couch amidst the torn wrapping paper.

Angel brought Ryan to his parents' house. He was so goddamn polite and happy, Angel thought his mom truly contemplated trading him for Ryan. Ryan was quite happy to lean against the sink, peeling potato after potato— Angel's most hated chore.

Angel's dad was a different matter. He pressed his lips together and creased his forehead, and Angel knew he wasn't completely comfortable with Angel's sexuality. He didn't think his dad was homophobic; he thought it would've been fine if he'd just been gay. But since he'd been with Alicia and had Finn, his dad seemed to think it wrong or weird for Angel to be with a guy now. He thought Finn should have a mom.

Angel knew, or at least hoped, he'd get over it eventually. His dad had always supported everything Angel had chosen to do, even if he would've much preferred Angel took another approach. He would've preferred Angel to have taken up football or basketball or baseball instead of painting in high school, and to have stayed in New York instead of uprooting his little family to move to Chicago to get his Master's and be closer to Finn's other set of grandparents. Angel hoped his preconceived notion of what a family was could be put away too.

In any event, it only took a few words from Ryan about the Giants' season to win his dad over. Ryan wondered aloud if they could defend their Superbowl championship, and right away, Mr. Posadas was grinning and rambling on about why the Giants might still have a chance. It was hardly full acceptance, but it was getting there. Maybe the way to Dad's heart was via someone he could actually talk sports with.

Nicola loved Ryan on sight because he was handsome and had a present tucked under his arm for her. Rosa already hero-worshipped him, which confused Angel, because she was strictly anti-military. It was probably his dynamic with Finn that won her over. The sisters and Ryan chatted, and Angel had no chance of sitting next to Ryan through dinner. He sat with his three-year-old nephew, Elijah's arm bumping his and Sara's intense gaze upon him. She'd barely been civil and had, consequently, received a few scornful looks from their mom and a hissed reminder about guests. He helped Sara, her husband Thomas, and Ryan clear the table, but Sara quickly ushered Thomas and Ryan to the living room to keep Elijah company.

She turned to face Angel with arms crossed. "So that's why you went out of your mind for months? That's what was worth terrifying mom and dad and me and Rosa?"

"You know he's a person, right? You can't refer to him as a 'what', Sara," Angel gritted out as he rinsed a dish and stacked it in the dishwasher.

"Answer me, Angel," Sara demanded.

"If you must know, yes, he's worth it."

"He better be good to you two."

"Better than I am to him."

That comment made Sara's face go soft, and she placed a hand on his forearm, freezing his motions.

"Oh, baby brother," she said, squeezing his arm and smiling sadly, "You're a catch, you know that, right?"

"You have to say that; you're my sister," he joked, a self-deprecating smile pulling at the corners of his mouth.

"Angel," she whispered, pulling him into a side hug. For such a slight woman, she sure knew how to make his ribs creak.

"I'm okay, Sara," he reassured her. "I am now, anyway."

There was no more talking after that. They left the kitchen with arms slung around each other, to a raised eyebrow from their mom. They exchanged gifts, and Angel thought the little gifts Ryan purchased for each member of his family were so personal and perfect and so much better than his own, even though he bought exactly what they asked for.

After all the wrapping paper was stuffed into trash bags, Nicola insisted they watch the stop-motion classics they loved as kids. Angel squeezed himself into a spot between Ryan and Rosa, who gave him a dirty look because she was clearly cold, and Ryan was a human furnace. He smirked at her and tucked himself into Ryan's side.

"How did you know what to buy everyone?" he murmured into Ryan's neck.

"You talk about them a lot."

"You listen to all of that?"

"Some of the time," Ryan joked.

Angel was a little in awe, but he tried to not let it show. As usual, he fell asleep through the movie, and he only woke up when Ryan shifted to go to the bathroom. They left shortly after that, and Ryan insisted on driving. Ryan drove exactly as Angel had expected: methodically and safely, as if he had a silent drill sergeant guiding his every move. Angel usually couldn't fall asleep when other people had his life in their hands, but he drifted off with his head pressed against the cold glass.

The next day, they went to pick up Finn at the airport. The flight was slightly delayed. Winter weather was shit, Angel thought with some hostility, yearning to see the little smiling face. The cold made him tired; He sought out the airport coffee shop and got himself the darkest, blackest coffee they had. He got Ryan a caramel macchiato because he knew Ryan really liked them but refused to order them for himself.

The line was so long, it was a fucking joke, but the baristas were whipping orders out faster than Angel thought people should legally be allowed to move, so he wasn't too concerned. Of course, it still took longer than expected, and the cashier looked relieved when he asked for a black coffee-of-the-day and a caramel macchiato, a nice easy order.

He sipped on his coffee as he ambled back to where Ryan was standing; they were still selling the Christmas blend, and it tasted like what Angel imagined a Christmas tree would taste if it were pureed and turned into a beverage. Oddly enough, he enjoyed it.

He stopped when he saw Ryan's uncomfortable stance and the man he was talking to. He approached quickly, wanting to save Ryan from the awkward conversation, but then slowed when he realized Ryan's stance wasn't awkward— it was military. Angel could feel his muscles tense and his pulse kick up a notch, which was why he didn't notice the five-year-old cannonball barrelling toward Ryan.

***

"Garry, is that you?" The words were a deep southern drawl.

Ryan's reaction was Pavlovian: His heartbeat skyrocketed, hands flew behind his back, and his feet widened; he turned quickly on his heels to face his future commanding officer— the man who would dictate where his career would go after desk duty.

"Colonel Adkins," Ryan said stiffly. His hand was itching to salute, but he wouldn't. It was neither necessary nor recommended to salute when in civvies, but he had to keep reminding his muscles that.

"Relax," Adkins said pleasantly with a smile on his face. Ryan tried to turn up his lips into something other than a grimace, but he could tell he wasn't really succeeding by the perturbed look on the older man's face. It wasn't that Adkins wasn't nice— Adkins was one of the most congenial men on the base— but he was also a "good ol' boy" who was very stuck in his traditional values.

Ryan prayed Angel would read the situation and stay away; he didn't, however, consider the younger Posadas. The one that started squeezing his healthy leg for dear life just as he went to ask Adkins how his day is going. Ryan looked down at Finn, whose full-wattage smile was hard to resist responding to. He grinned as best he could, but it was shaky, and Finn's smile turned iffy. Adkins looked confused, and Ryan felt his chest filling with dread.

A moment later, Finn was being dragged off Ryan's leg by a determined Angel. Adkins's eyebrows knit further together, expression going from confused to disturbed, and Ryan wanted very much to disappear into the crowd, never to be seen again.

"Thanks for coming to pick us up," Angel was saying. "Glad I chose you to be his godfather."

Finn looked up at Angel confusedly and moved to say something, but Angel placed his hand on Finn's head and he froze. Ryan smiled stiffly and nodded.

143

Adkins's face crinkled a little bit, but he seemed to accept the situation as proposed.

"Well, Garry, I need to be getting to the family," Adkins said. "I look forward to seeing you in the New Year."

"Yes sir, I look forward to it too," Ryan replied.

When Adkins walked away, Ryan and Angel's shoulders sagged in unison. Finn looked at them both bewilderedly, his enthusiasm dampened. He pressed himself against Angel's side, turning his face into Angel and away from Ryan. Ryan felt a physical ache, wanting to swing Finn up into his arms, kiss his forehead, and tell him how damn important he was. He'd always loved kids; it was part of why he tried so hard and for so long to be straight, if he was honest with himself. He probably could take Finn from Angel and not draw any attention to them, but the anxious pull in his chest and his throbbing leg kept him from doing it. He did venture to ruffle Finn's hair, and it earned him a tentative grin.

They went back to Angel's apartment without speaking much, and Finn's excitement returned when he saw the stack of presents around the tiny fake tree. They opened presents, and Ryan loved watching Finn zip through the stack while Angel rested his hand on Ryan's thigh. Finn thanked them for the presents and crawled into each of their laps to give them a snuggle.

Next, Angel opened the present that was sent from Chicago in Finn's bag for him, and his face dropped a little, but he didn't explain, and Ryan didn't want to pry. Later, Finn fell asleep on the couch, his head in Angel's lap and his feet in Ryan's, and Ryan thought he might get a chance to speak to Angel about what happened earlier. Only then, Angel, fell asleep too with his head on Ryan's shoulder.

God, it was all such a mess. Ryan didn't want to give this up. From the moment he met Angel, he knew that, for some reason, this was the person who would give him what he'd been missing in life; he also knew he needed to preserve his career. Before everything, Ryan was a soldier. So tomorrow, he'd go back to his apartment on base and only visit Angel and Finn. He couldn't continue to be so reckless, not after today; Adkins could have easily figured out what was going on. In fact, if he had been there twenty minutes earlier, he would've caught Ryan with his hand in Angel's pocket. That terrified Ryan. He was not reckless by nature. He needed to stop; he needed to extract himself from the situation, pull away, and add that distance and caution back into their relationship. It wasn't ideal, but Ryan couldn't see any other way around it.

The movie ended and he picked Finn up and tucked him into bed. Angel had awoken a little bit, but he was still very pliant and bleary-eyed. Contentment showed on Angel's face, and Ryan tried to return it. They headed to the master bedroom where Angel undressed languidly. Angel helped Ryan take his shirt off, dropping easy kisses in between his shoulder blades. Ryan felt himself tensing despite himself, and

Angel looked at him, concern creeping into his languorous expression.

"I think I'm going to go back to my place tomorrow," Ryan said, hesitantly.

"What? Why?" Angel demanded, fully awake now.

"I just think I'm getting too comfortable here, and eventually, I'm going to have to go back to base."

"You don't have to go back."

Ryan sighed. "Angel, not this again."

"It's true, though, that you don't have to go back."

"I have to go back; I have a job to do."

Angel tossed his head and frowned at a fixed spot on the wall. "Then you should just leave now, right? Why wait?"

Ryan's chest clenched. "Angel, I know you're angry."

"I'm not angry; it's just if you're going to leave, you might as well get on with it."

"Tomorrow is just as good a day as any," Ryan reasoned.

"Leave!" Angel shouted suddenly. "Just fucking leave."

"Come on, Angel!" Ryan felt urgent now, aching all over with uncertainty and distress, not knowing how to put it right. "You knew this would happen."

"You promised two months; I don't want someone around who is too much of a coward to keep a promise. So get the fuck out."

That was final enough. Ryan didn't say anything else; he just grabbed the most essential things he needed and shoved them haphazardly into his duffel. He grabbed his wallet and keys off the table by the front door and put on his pea coat.

"Give me the key," Angel demanded.

Ryan felt bile rise in his throat and clenched the keys closer to his chest instinctively. Angel's face was angry, his lips pressed together and his hand held out stiffly. Ryan's hands shook as he tried to remove the key from the ring. His fingernails weren't long enough, and he couldn't open the ring to slide the key around it. Angel's foot began to tap obnoxiously. He finally got the key around the ring, placed it in Angel's outstretched hand, and pressed Angel's fingers over it. For a second, he saw the flat expression on Angel's face crack, but a moment later, the impassive anger was back in full-force.

It was a long agonizing trip back to Ryan's apartment, and when he got there, he absolutely regretted saying anything. His apartment felt stale; he'd barely spent five hours there since he came back. It didn't have the warmth of lived-in places. It didn't have the gentle scent of Angel's cologne and the citrus shampoo everyone in the apartment used. He opened the windows, even though it was below freezing, and let in the fresh air.

He wallowed in his sweats, his comforter wrapped around his shoulders and takeout cartons stacking up by the sofa. He didn't go out on New Year's Eve because the only people in the city he wanted to be with didn't want him around, and instead, he rang in the New Year watching the ball drop on TV while he ate an entire frozen pizza and drank an entire bottle of champagne.

On the second, his phone rang. "THE GREAT T RILEY," flashed across the screen— Travis' doing, not his. His hands shook a little; the only time Travis had ever called him was when Angel's phone died when they were out. He was expecting to get reamed.

"Hello?" he answered hesitantly.

"Ryan?" It wasn't the voice he'd expected at all. It was Finn, and Ryan's chest clenched.

"Yeah, bud, it's me. How are you?"

"I miss you." Finn's voice cracked a little and Ryan's heart sank.

"Oh, buddy, I miss you so much."

"Why did you leave?"

"It had nothing to do with you. Your dad and I had a disagreement."

"But he misses you too."

"And I miss him."

"Then come home."

Ryan felt the tears well in his eyes and knew: It really was home. This place was no longer his home. The boxy two-bedroom apartment in Queens had taken that title.

"It's not that easy."

Finn really started crying then. Full sobs that got further away as he put the phone down, and it was picked up by another person, presumably Travis.

"I was expecting you to cheer him up," Travis said harshly.

"I'm sorry."

"Goddamn, you two are fucking idiots."

"Watch your language," Ryan snapped and Travis laughed.

"You sound like Angel," Travis said.

Ryan sucked in a breath.

"He wants to see you; we only have a few more hours until Angel is done at the studio. Want to meet us in Chinatown for lunch?"

He hadn't showered in three days. He looked like absolute shit, and he knew it, but, nonetheless, he said, "Absolutely."

It took him nearly an hour, and he hated wasting this time. He bounced his good leg the entire trip, irritating the shit out of whoever had the misfortune to sit by him. When he got to the restaurant, Travis and Finn were waiting outside. Finn ran full force at him, and Ryan didn't care that his leg twinged when Finn plowed into him. He swung Finn up into his arms. Finn pressed his face into Ryan's neck and he kissed the boy's hair. He could feel his neck getting wet and he rubbed the shaking back. Travis looked on judgmentally, but every second that went by, Ryan could see him soften.

They had a wonderful meal, and Finn told him all about what he'd been doing for the last week. Travis promised to set up meetings and let them hang out. Finn seemed so relieved, and Ryan felt horrible. He wanted to just go home with him and see Angel, and he wanted to stay there forever. He wanted to see them every day, wanted Finn to be his son as much as he was Angel's. Wanted Angel to be his partner in everything. Now, that aspiration seemed so far away.

Two days later, there was a knock on his door. Ryan wasn't sure who to expect. This time, it was Mike. He was scuffing his boots and grimaced a little when Ryan opened the door.

"I've been sent to check on you."

Ryan laughed shortly. "I'm alright."

"Are you? I sure wouldn't be."

"You know I'm just saying that."

"I do," Mike said wryly, and Ryan sighed.

"Mike, what's really going on?"

"Why won't you just go back?"

"It's not that easy."

"Yeah, it is; I think he would take you right back."

"He wants me to choose between him and my career; I can't do that."

Mike eyed him intensely. "Why not?"

"Would you?"

"What?"

"If you had to choose between being a chef and Travis, what would you choose?"

Mike didn't miss a beat. "Travis, one hundred and ten percent."

"Fuck you, Mike."

"It's true," Mike said. "I mean, not that I wouldn't be a little mad if he asked me to choose," he admitted. Ryan really had to think. While Mike would choose Travis, that's also because Mike could do something else. Ryan didn't have that option.

"Mike, I'm not good at anything else."

"Bullshit," Mike said immediately. "You're one of the most resourceful people I know; you would figure something else out easily. But the thing is, he's not even asking you to choose yet. He's just asking you to be less scared. He wants to know you love him more than the job."

Mike stayed for a little bit longer, but he seemed to have spoken his peace and left to go to work.

On the twentieth, Ryan had the same nervousness as he always did on his first day of a new rotation. The desk job was going to be extremely boring, but everyone seemed easy to work with. It wouldn't be as bad as he thought. It would at least take his mind off Angel and Finn.

His phone rang when he was typing up some paperwork. It was Angel's number, and Ryan was confused by why he'd call now. He wondered if this was some kind of test, and he determinedly decided not to answer. He let it go to voicemail, and it only took five minutes before his phone started exploding with notifications. He got missed calls from Angel, Mike, Travis, and Rosa, followed by an assortment of cryptic texts. They all just read, "Pick up your phone."

So when it said, "Angel calling," again across the screen, he picked up. Angel's breathing was wrecked, and Ryan was positive he'd been crying without even hearing any words.

"Hello?"

"Get your ass to New York Hospital Queens," Angel ordered, his voice unhinged.

"Why? What happened, Angel? It's my first day; I can't just leave for no reason," Ryan pointed out. Angel laughed brokenly on the other end of the line, and it was more terrifying than any noise Ryan had ever heard.

"Fuck you," Angel snapped, and then the connection went dead.

Chapter Eleven

The pillow smacked Angel squarely in the face, and he just blinked. If he ignored Travis, maybe he'd stop and just go away. Go back to his stupid little love-nest with his stupid curly boyfriend and leave him to revel in self-pity and consuming hatred while he ate chicken nuggets and watched cartoons.

"This is the fourth time I've watched this show with you this week," Travis whined.

"Fucking leave, then," Angel growled.

"That's what you said to him, too, huh?" Travis prodded, and Angel wondered if he was bored and looking for a fight.

"I swear, Trav. You need to get the fuck out of here."

"Stop being a prick."

"He could call," Angel pointed out.

"You kicked him out and demanded back your key because he was going back to his apartment. Tell me where that told him if he called, you would answer."

Angel made a strangled noise. "When the fuck did you decide to be on his side?"

"I'm on your side, Angel; I'm always on yours and Finn's side. You know that."

"Then why are you excusing his behavior?"

Travis sighed. "I'm not; he's a little bitch-ass coward, but he loves you and Finn."

"How do you know that?"

"Finn and I hung out with him while you were at the studio. I'm far more cynical than you, and even I could see it. He held Finn like Finn was his son. I… you… you guys can't lose him, A."

Angel walked out of the room straightaway because, while he was worried his fist might become more closely acquainted with Travis' face, he was also worried he might break down in tears. He promised himself he wouldn't be sad this time, that he would hold onto the anger and let that fester. He wasn't going to cry and worry Finn. He was going to be angry. Anger had always been easier for him to control and hide than sadness. He stood in the kitchen staring at the contents of his fridge until Travis approached him like a man stalking a dangerous animal.

"You're not going to hit me, right? Because I need this face for performances. And Mike kind of likes this face, and he's been doing some boxing recently. I'd prefer if my boyfriend and best friend didn't get into it, especially since you would probably lose, and that would be awkward all around," Travis rambled.

"Shut up, Travis," Angel said quietly. Travis nodded and Angel couldn't look at him.

"You know that's your tell, right?"

"Huh?"

"Your soulful little eyes have always been incredible about making eye contact, at least with me, except when you know you've fucked up."

Angel sighed. "Of course I know I've fucked up. I just can't play second fiddle to some archaic, inane

154

system that controls him. He'll choose the military, and we don't know how long this stupid law is going to be in place. I want to get married again, Travis, and have a proper family. He made me realize that for the first time after Alicia, but it's like he offered it, and then took it away. We can't be a family if we're constantly hiding."

"Okay," Travis accepted and pulled Angel in for a hug. Angel relaxed into Travis, and maybe Travis' shirt was a little damper when he pulled away.

Angel had to convince Rosa to come babysit Finn for the rest of the break. She didn't seem that reluctant, though, happy to sleep on the trundle in Finn's room since it was only for a few days. Angel knew that Rosa and Travis had started taking Finn to see Ryan. He knew that when he worked at the studio, Travis, Ryan, and Finn usually went on some sort of outing. In his weakness, he felt torn between two extremes: forbidding this, or begging to join in. He knew he couldn't do either. He didn't want to upset Finn again, but he couldn't put himself out there that way, either.

He'd thrown himself instead into his work, and he'd been told on numerous occasions recently that he seemed almost manic. He'd gotten a lot more done, but it almost seemed worthless, because he didn't exude the calm energy that made him good at his job. Everyone could feel the tension rolling off of him, and most of his sessions had been legitimate shit.

Within weeks of going back to school, Finn got a cold. Angel wrinkled his nose. Schools were basically just large petri dishes. He made sure he had plenty of fluids and tissues out for Finn. Finn got super clingy, too, and whined about everything he had to do, so Angel rented his favorite movies to placate him. At night, he'd just lay on Angel until he fell asleep, occasionally whining that he wanted Ryan to be around because he was more comfy to lie on. Despite himself, Angel remembered how it felt to curl up with his cheek on Ryan's broad chest and sighed. The kid was right.

One night, over the long MLK weekend, Finn crawled into bed with Angel and pressed his sweaty body against his, his little limbs shivering. Angel felt like a horrible parent these days, especially when Finn asked for Ryan, and then again when Angel couldn't take a day off to be with him because he'd already taken off too many days. So, when Finn didn't seem better after the long weekend, Angel called and asked his mom if she could come watch him. She promised to be there by seven, and he thanked her with genuine gratitude.

In the morning, he went to check on Finn and found him still feverish and coughing. He gave him more children's ibuprofen, helped him change into a new pair of pajamas, made him drink more water, and kissed his forehead. His mom shooed him off to work, telling him not to worry; that kids got sick all the time, and that she'd take him to the doctor if he was still ill tomorrow.

He was preoccupied much of the day, checking his phone for text messages on Finn's wellbeing from his mom. He got an all-clear text message at ten and then left his phone on his desk to go into a two-hour session. He came back to three missed calls, all from twenty minutes or so after he'd left, which sent him into an instant panic. He called back with shaking fingers.

"Hello?" came the weary answer.

"Mom?" Angel's heart was pounding. "What's wrong?"

"I need you to sit down."

That had the opposite of a calming effect. "What happened?"

"He's going to be all right."

"Oh, f–" Angel bit his lip. "Just tell me. Please."

"I had to call an ambulance, Angel; he passed out in the middle of the living room while he was walking to the bathroom. When I rushed over to him, he was burning up. We're at New York Hospital Queens. He's been asking for you and Ryan."

"I'll be there as soon as I can," Angel promised, and he thought that, if his stomach wasn't empty, he would vomit. He informed his supervisor, who let him go right away. He ran out to his car as quickly as he could. It wasn't until he was trying to scroll through his contacts that he realized he was crying.

He called Travis and his sisters. His sisters already knew and were on their way, and he could hear Travis start getting ready immediately, even before Angel was done explaining the situation. Angel drove to the hospital at inadvisable speeds, throwing his car into the first parking spot he saw. Inside, his mom was pacing near the pediatric emergency room, and she sagged when she saw him. She pulled him into a hug, and Angel wished he could stay in the embrace forever, be ten again with none of this to worry about.

When they separated, she took him to a room filled with the low beeping of machines. A tangle of tubes led down to a small figure on the bed. His eyes were closed in a fitful sleep, and Angel needed to touch him to make sure he was alive, even though the gentle beeping of the heart monitor was a constant reminder. His eyes fluttered open when Angel's hand rested on his damp forehead.

"Daddy?" he asked softly, his eyes struggling to focus on Angel's face.

"Yeah," Angel said breathlessly.

"I don't feel very good."

"I see that."

"I'm happy you came; I was scared."

Angel bit his lip. "I'm sorry, baby."

"S'okay."

"Is there anything I can do to make you feel better?"

"Can you call Ryan and Uncle Travis and Aunt Rosa and Aunt Sara and Aunt Nicola? I want to see them."

The order of names made Angel wince, but he fought to collect himself. "Aunt Nicola is in the waiting room with Grandma and Grandpa. Aunt Rosa, Sara, and Uncle Travis are on their way."

"What about Ryan?"

"I'll call him."

"Thanks, Daddy. I'm going to go back to sleep now 'cause I'm tired."

He closed his eyes again and Angel pushed his hair back. He went out into the waiting room, where his mom told him gently that he'd been diagnosed with bacterial pneumonia. The doctors were pretty positive he'd be well after a round of antibiotics and lots of fluids and rest, but left at home, he could easily have died.

***

"Fuck," Ryan spat under his breath, fumbling with his phone in his haste to call Angel back. Angel didn't pick up. Ryan finally processed the phone call. The realization that it was about Finn hit him sharply. Angel wouldn't call for himself. How was Ryan going to leave without bringing attention to himself? It was three, and the day wasn't supposed to end until five. He tried to figure out his escape plan. He couldn't wait two hours to go to the hospital; he'd never be forgiven. He finished the paperwork on his desk as quickly as possible and rushed to Colonel Adkins's office.

"Sir," he ventured, knocking on the door. "I've completed all the paperwork."

"Good God, Garry, that's at least two days of work. I thought it would take you all week," Adkins said in amusement. "You must be feeling it."

"Yes, sir," he reported.

"Well, go home Garry. There's nothing else for you to do today," Adkins said. "I might have expected someone with a broken femur to beg off before now, anyway."

Ryan tried to call Angel again, but he didn't pick up. No matter. It was a short enough bus ride to the nearest car rental; it would be over a hundred dollars to rent a car for one day, but Ryan wasn't about to spend two hours on public transport right now. When he finished the paperwork for the car rental, he climbed into the car and called Mike. He figured he'd be the most sympathetic and might actually pick up his phone.

"Hello?" Mike whispered into the phone.

"Hey, are you still at the hospital?"

"Yes. You're an idiot."

"I know."

"You made Angel cry."

"I'm sorry. He took the phone call the wrong way."

"No, you responded the wrong way. You didn't just say 'all right, I'll be there.' You asked what was wrong. You brought up your stupid job. The word 'hospital' should have sufficed. And as angry as we all want to be with you, Finn is asking for you."

Ryan sighed. "I'm coming; I got a rental car."

"Good," Mike said as he clicked off the phone.

It still took him nearly an hour to get to Queens, but he liked being in control. He liked knowing he was doing all he could to get there as fast as he could. He rushed into the hospital, skidded to the front desk, and they pointed him in the direction of the pediatric unit.

He saw the entire Posadas family in the waiting room with Travis and Mike. Travis and Sara shot daggers at him instantly. Angel wasn't there, but he walked in a few moments later, talking about how Finn was getting settled in his room. Then, his eyes landed on Ryan and the rage ignited in his face.

"Get out," he hissed.

"No," Ryan responded firmly.

"Get out, get out, get out," Angel chanted as he stalked up to Ryan and started shoving him bodily out of the unit.

"I'm sorry," Ryan pleaded, and Angel started beating on his chest. It hurt, but it was no longer meant to get him to leave. Angel's fists pounded uselessly on his chest, and he was sobbing. Ryan wrapped his arms around Angel's flailing limbs and pulled him closer, even though Angel seemed intent on hurting him. After a few seconds, the punching stopped and Angel pressed his face into Ryan's neck, his hands pinned between their bodies. The feeling of Angel's fingers curling into his shirt made Ryan's chest throb thickly, and he cupped the back of Angel's head, closing his eyes as he held him.

"Angel, I'm so sorry. God, you don't even know how sorry I am. I was shocked and I responded like an idiot."

"He wants to see you," Angel whispered. "You're the first person he asked me to call, and you brushed it off."

"I'm sorry."

"I can't go in like this. It'll upset him," Angel said, scrubbing his hand over his face.

"Come on, we'll go to the restroom, and then go in to see him. Everyone else can go in right now."

They went into the restroom together, and Angel splashed water on his face. Ryan reached out for him and then put his hands in his pockets.

"Angel, I want you to know that I love you. I know you don't think that, but I do. I didn't know what was happening when you called. I'm terrified of all this. I'm terrified of being in love. I'm terrified of having a child who relies on me. I'm terrified of losing my job. I'm just plain terrified."

Angel's face was impassive. "So am I."

"But I realized that I'm more terrified of losing the two of you than anything else."

"You swear?"

"I swear." Ryan bit his lip.

"I still need some time. Okay?"

"Okay."

Angel turned and pushed him against the wall of the restroom. For a moment, Ryan anticipated more violence, but then Angel slid his hands up under Ryan's shirt and kissed him. Completely relieved, Ryan gripped the back of Angel's neck, mouthing at his lips until Angel pulled away, breathing hard, his hands still on the small of Ryan's back.

"We can keep trying, right?"

"Yeah," Ryan said firmly. "I won't put my job first again."

Angel nodded. Ryan could tell he didn't really believe what he was being told. Angel thought, that until Ryan quit, he'd always be inadvertently putting the military first. That wasn't something Ryan could deal with right now. There were more important, pressing matters.

They walked into Finn's room together, their fingers tentatively linked. Finn let out a wheezy shout that sent him into a coughing fit. Ryan frowned and Angel wrung his hands, but Finn's glowing smile made them loosen a little. Ryan perched himself on the edge of the bed near Finn's head, and Finn wiggled so he was pressed against him. He sighed into the warmth and whispered, "I want you to stay here with me."

"I can do that, buddy," Ryan said, running his fingers through Finn's sweaty hair. The rest of the room froze and turned to look at Angel, but Angel only nodded in response.

Chapter Twelve

The doctors said Finn needed at least three days of bed rest, so Angel called his school and let them know. The teacher offered to email over some information about what they'd be covering, but assured Angel he wouldn't be far behind, even if he didn't finish the work. Finn only spent one night in the hospital to make sure the antibiotics were making an impact. Angel's mom offered to stay with them because Angel couldn't afford to take too many days off. All of this made it harder to accept Ryan back into their realm. Angel didn't want to give over responsibility to somebody who might not be around.

Angel only took off the day they brought Finn home from the hospital. When he got home on Friday night, he was expecting to find his mom on the couch with a book and Finn taking a nap. It was frightening to Angel how much Finn had been sleeping since he got sick. His little boy who would usually do anything not to sleep was now willingly going to his bedroom to take one or two naps a day.

Instead of finding his mom, though, he found Finn asleep on Ryan's lap. Ryan was running his hand slowly over Finn's back, flicking through the TV channels with his other hand. He smiled at Angel, and Angel tried to return it, but the warmth that coursed through him was paralyzing. He walked to the kitchen, confused by the sight. It was what he wanted to see: Ryan must have taken off early to be there now, but he wondered if it would last. He called his mom.

"Hello, sunshine."

"Hi, Mom."

"Did you call about Ryan?"

"Yeah."

"Darling, you know I would never leave Finn with someone I didn't trust implicitly. You have to let that boy back in. I know it's hard, and he'll probably hurt you again. It'll probably be really difficult, but nothing is easy, darling. At least, nothing that's worth your time. Your relationship with Alicia was easy. If you thought that was better than you and Ryan, you are so far in denial, I don't know what will save you."

Angel pressed a hand to his face. "Mom, this whole military thing just gets to me."

"It's his job, Angel. You have to understand how he must feel about it. It was his goal since he was fifteen; his career has been his top priority for years. You can't make him choose. You have to hope that he chooses you two over the military, but not force him to leave it. In the end, I think given the choice, he'll choose the two of you, but you have to know that giving someone an ultimatum never works out."

Angel let out a heavy sigh, and his mom chuckled softly. She said, "Go into the living room," and he sighed again, but followed her direction. He stood where he couldn't be seen, but where he still had a good vantage point of where Ryan and Finn were sitting. In his ear, his mom's voice said, "Think about what you see. Is that something you'd like to see more of? I want you to think about how you are feeling when you see those two together, and I want

165

you to stop hesitating because you're scared that you might care more about him than he does about you."

"Mom," Angel began.

"And I know that you were trying to sneak him in and out without me noticing, late in the evenings and early in the mornings, but in case you forgot, I've raised four teenagers."

Angel sputtered but didn't see the point in denying it.

"I love you," she said.

"I love you too."

He hung up and leaned against the doorframe. He couldn't look away from Ryan, who seemed completely content to have Finn sprawled over him as he watched a football rerun. Ryan leaned down unconsciously and kissed Finn's forehead gently, checking his temperature. Ryan never seemed to make mistakes like Angel did when Finn was born, and he wasn't nearly as awkward as Angel was. Angel remembered Alicia giving him Finn the first time and how awkwardly he'd held him.

He knew his awkwardness had come from the responsibility weighing on him. Every time he had held Finn for the first two weeks of his life, Finn had screamed bloody murder. Alicia had been pretty understanding, but after getting only five hours of sleep in fifty hours, she lost it. She had demanded he take Finn so she could sleep for a full night. He had spent an hour with Finn squirming and crying against him. He was glad nobody was there to see him give into his tears and cry with his son for over twenty minutes. After that, it had gotten easier. However, it wasn't nearly as easy as Ryan was making it look.

He walked back into the living room and sat next to Ryan on the couch, reaching out to check Finn's temperature. He was warm, but not burning up like he had been earlier in the week; just sleep-warm. Ryan lifted his arm up and placed it around Angel's shoulders, like it was the most natural thing in the world.

Angel shook Finn's shoulder tentatively to ask, "What do you want for dinner?"

"Chicken noodle soup?" Finn croaked, and Angel nodded. He felt the smile tug at his mouth because this was the first time Finn hadn't said "nothing" in two weeks.

"I'll make it," Ryan said, shifting Finn into Angel's lap. Finn curled into Angel's body heat, and Angel ran his fingers through his dark locks. Angel liked this ability to split responsibilities, so that he didn't have to leave Finn alone on the couch, especially when Finn hummed happily at being cuddled.

The soup was delicious, and Angel could see Finn getting better by the minute. He hoped that by the middle of next week, he'd be able to send him back to school. After the soup, Finn begged for a movie, but fell asleep twenty minutes in.

Afterward, they sat together on the couch, and Angel took the opportunity to look at Ryan without interruption. Ryan looked contented, and Angel knew he was healing well. He'd be out of his cast soon and starting physical therapy. Angel worried that he'd have to go back to his tour. He couldn't manage that. He didn't want him to go back now.

The next morning, Ryan told Angel that his mom was going to drive his car over from the Midwest, explaining that he needed his car to be able to come see them more often. Angel couldn't stop smiling the entire day, even when Paul demanded new paintings, and he had to spend most of his Saturday at the studio instead of home with Ryan and Finn.

***

Colonel Adkins called Ryan into his office halfway through his desk duty, and he had an intense internal freak-out. He didn't know what it was regarding, but he hoped it was nothing negative. He hoped Adkins hadn't figured out where he was going most weekends and some nights. He walked in and stood at attention until Adkins finished the papers he was working on.

"At ease, Garry," Adkins said. "I have a bone to pick with you."

"Okay," Ryan said tentatively, his heart rate making it hard to hear.

"Why didn't you tell me you had a degree in Civil Engineering?"

"I'm sorry, sir; I thought you knew."

"Well, I didn't, and I've been wasting your talents on menial paperwork."

Ryan could hardly believe his ears. "I thought that's what desk duty was supposed to be about. I wasn't expecting to get an engineering project; I thought those were only for warrant officers."

"Garry, you have all the qualifications to be a warrant officer if you want."

"I'm not sure if that's where I want to go, sir."

Adkins smiled good-naturedly. "That's how I was, too— wanted to always protect my country physically. Thought fighting was more important than the other tasks."

"I didn't mean it that way."

"Not the point. The point is, when I met my wife, I decided that maybe she was more important than going off to fight. I've noticed that you have someone you care about; it's hard to miss with the way you take your lunch breaks in private and spend the time on the phone smiling. Just take it into consideration, Garry. I would be happy to have you."

"Thank you, sir."

He was surprised by the offer, and that Adkins had figured out that he had a significant other. He had thought he was being discreet, but he wasn't too concerned, because Adkins didn't seem suspicious at all. If Adkins thought Ryan had a girlfriend, maybe that was all good.

He had to go to physical therapy that night, but afterward, he drove to Queens. When he arrived, Finn was already in pajamas. He launched himself at Ryan and expounded upon how excited he was to be going to Myrtle Beach for spring break. Ryan agreed, and Finn made Ryan tell him everything they were going to do at Myrtle Beach again. Angel sighed indulgently and told Finn that he needed to get in bed. Finn sighed over-dramatically and, as a compromise, both Angel and Ryan had to read him a story.

When they left Finn's room, Angel caught Ryan by surprise, pressed him against the wall, and kissed him fiercely. His hand curved against the front of Ryan's jeans, and Ryan almost forgot about the promotion he'd meant to discuss with Angel. They hadn't found the time to do this properly in a while, and now, Ryan's cock was standing at attention, a better soldier than Ryan had ever been. When Ryan pulled back from the kiss, Angel made a toe-curling noise in the back of his throat.

"I'm horny," Angel moaned into Ryan's neck.

"We need to talk," Ryan said, even as his palms slid down Angel's back to his hips, pulling their bodies flush.

"That sounds ominous," Angel responded, rolling his hips in a slow grind. "Don't want ominous, want amorous."

Ryan laughed. Fuck. *Be strong, Garry.* "Come on, Angel, this is serious. I'll let you do anything you want after we talk about this."

Angel's face lit up, and Ryan almost regretted that offer. "Anything I want?"

"Well, within reason, Angel."

Angel huffed, but seemed to decide he'd take his chances and led them to the living room. He pushed Ryan into the chair, and Ryan assumed Angel would take a seat on the couch to avoid distraction, but he didn't seem too committed, slinging one leg over Ryan's thighs and seating himself in his lap. "Speak."

"I'm not a dog."

"Ryan, get the fuck on with it."

Ryan bit his lip. "I've been offered a raise."

"Good for you," Angel sighed, like he didn't care. "It's still military."

"But it'll be mostly a desk job. I might have to ship out, but I'll never be in direct combat again."

That caught Angel's attention, stilled his hips. "No more suicide bombers?"

"Well, I can't completely remove it from the list, but for the most part, yeah, no more suicide bombers. I'll be far off the front lines, and I'll be using my degree from West Point."

"You've never told me what you have a degree in."

"Civil Engineering."

Angel's eyes widened. "Wait, what the fuck? You could get a job anywhere."

Ryan shrugged. "I guess."

"You guess?"

"Angel, I thought this would be good for us."

Angel rolled his eyes. "Getting a job outside of the army would be good for us. For fuck's sake, Ryan, you could be making way more than you're making now."

"Yeah, but I wouldn't be protecting my nation."

"The nation that won't let you be who you are? The nation that makes us have to hide? The nation that will fire you from your job because you like to suck my dick?"

Ryan looked away. Once again, he shouldn't have said a word. "Angel, forget I said anything; I thought it would make you happy. I'm sorry, you can do whatever it is you wanted."

"My libido seems to have receded," Angel said tartly.

"Do you want me to leave?"

"Fuck, Ryan, I'm not going to do that anymore. I'm not going to kick you out every time we fight."

"Okay." Ryan's voice was small.

"I think I'm going to go to bed."

"Okay."

Ryan waited another hour before heading to the master bedroom. Angel was lying with his body turned away from Ryan's side of the bed, and every so often, he softly hiccupped, like someone who fell asleep in tears. It made Ryan feel regretful, and he felt the ache of unshed tears thick in his jaw.

Angel woke him up the next morning with soft kisses along his neck. They felt like an apology, a suspicion confirmed by what he said. "If you need to be part of the military, I'd rather you be the safest you can be."

Ryan flipped to face Angel, and his face was sincere. He kissed him softly at first, but Angel's fingers tightened in Ryan's t-shirt. The kiss swiftly deepened into something hot and fierce, with all of Ryan's gratitude in it.

"Morning breath gets more and more unattractive the longer you're with someone," Angel said as he pulled away. Ryan's uncharacteristic giggle startled Angel. They went to the bathroom, brushed their teeth, and climbed into the shower. They stayed in the shower until the water ran cold, Angel's head thrown back against the tiles and the water cascading down his throat as Ryan fucked him, fingers digging into his hips hard enough to leave bruises.

"God, Angel," Ryan murmured, sucking marks into that pale throat, "I want—"

"Yeah," Angel said as if he understood, clenching his muscles around Ryan's dick and hooking his calf more firmly around his waist. "Me too."

***

Ryan accepted Adkins's offer, and they talked about his options. He'd get more money, and his housing options would open up, too. Being an officer would mean he had permission to move off base. Ryan looked at the Basic Allowance for Housing and remembered the sign hanging on the door to Angel's apartment building about an apartment for rent.

Chapter Thirteen

This was the first time Angel had seen Ryan in nearly a week, except for the five minutes he saw him at the studio when he picked Finn up so Angel could paint. He knew that this new job was stressful for him. He was just learning the ropes, and it would cool down when he was no longer trying to play catch-up, but Angel really just wanted to tie him up on his bed and leave him there. Right now, Ryan and Finn were sitting at the small dining table in the corner of the living-dining room combo. Finn's face was concentrated as Ryan explained how to know if you should use addition or subtraction in a word problem. They made up a chart of words, separating them into addition and subtraction columns. Ryan was patient as ever, knowing just the right tone to use to keep Finn from getting frustrated.

"Are you sure you don't want to have your own kids one day?" Angel asked Ryan.

Ryan looked up at him and rolled his eyes. "What are you doing?"

"Asking you a question."

"Sounds more like picking a fight."

"I just think you'd be an amazing dad, and you should get the chance to do that."

"Are you saying adoption is out of the question?"

Angel shrugged. "I don't know if we could afford it, and it's an arduous process."

Ryan looked at him for a minute, and then laughed. "I wasn't talking about another child, though

I wouldn't be completely against that. I was talking about Finn."

"What?" Angel's heartbeat thundered in his ears. His first reaction was 'No,' and that wasn't because he didn't love Ryan, didn't think he'd make a wonderful dad. He didn't want to share Finn. *He* was Finn's dad. He was scared of letting Ryan push him out.

"I've thought about, maybe sometime in the future, marrying you," Ryan said softly, "and adopting Finn." The words were so matter-of-fact. Angel couldn't align them mentally with the guy he'd met who'd never sucked a dick before because of his terror of admitting to his own sexuality.

"But, but we can't," he stammered.

"Well, yeah, not right now, but the country is getting more progressive, and I think this government will make a lot of difference."

Angel took a deep breath. "Do you really want to do all those things?"

"Yeah, of course, but first, I think we should just talk about our living arrangements."

"What about them?"

Ryan smiled. "I saw the sign that there's an apartment for rent in the building."

"Yeah, right down the hall. It's a studio where some young teacher lives."

"Well, I have a BAH now, and I want to be near you guys."

"But a studio is too small for you," Angel pointed out.

"I was thinking I wouldn't spend a lot of time there, maybe keep it around for when Rosa needs a place to stay when she comes to babysit Finn. I also need to have an excuse to be in this building overnight so frequently."

"You mean…"

"I mean I'm inviting myself to live with you," Ryan declared, his cheeks flushing and his eyes dropping to his toes.

"Oh, fuck, Ryan, fuck," Angel said, and he tilted Ryan's chin up and kissed him hard. He nipped at Ryan's lower lip and Ryan's returning moan made Angel pull away. "Where's Finn?"

"I think he went to his room."

"We need to feed him and get him to bed before we do anything else."

"That's probably true," Ryan said, but he pulled Angel closer and nipped at his stubbly jaw.

"Fuck, don't do that; I'll forget I have a kid that needs to be fed and tucked in," Angel groaned as Ryan moved to the tender part of his neck. Ryan snorted into his skin, and Angel ran his hand into the grown-out buzz cut. He felt the giggle roll up his throat and burst over the top of Ryan's head. Ryan, in turn, smiled into Angel's neck and his humid laugh made Angel squirm.

There was a heavy sigh from the hallway, and Finn stood there with his fists on his hips. "I'm hungry."

"Yes, sir," Ryan said, straightening up and saluting at Finn, who only narrowed his eyes at them and then made a "move along" gesture that had Angel burying his face in Ryan's shirt to stifle his chuckle.

"I want grilled cheese and tomato soup," Finn demanded, as if perfectly used to ordering around people two decades older than him.

"Whoa, there, do we get a 'please?' "

Finn let out a put upon sigh. "Please."

"I'm not letting you spend as much time with Uncle Travis," Angel said, throwing Finn into the air. "I do not like this sass master monster that he's created."

"Uncle Travis says a little sass never hurt anyone," Finn declared when Angel put him down. He ran to the kitchen. "I want to help."

"Until I hurt him over it," Angel mumbled for Ryan's ears only, and Ryan chuckled heartily.

Finn got out the ingredients and helped make the sandwiches with too many slices of cheese before Ryan put them on the griddle. Angel heated up the organic tomato and red pepper soup he got from the local co-operative market. The three of them were standing with their hips pressed together with Finn on a stool between them, and Angel couldn't help but notice how easy it felt. Ryan held an arm in front of Finn's chest when he got a little too excited, and Angel handed him the wooden spoon to let him help stir so he could avoid the searing metal griddle and popping butter.

They ate while Finn chattered on about his day. Ryan asked Finn follow-up after follow-up question, and Angel just watched the enthusiasm wash over them. He could see the genuine interest in Ryan's eyes and mutual affection between them. He added his own questions, and Finn answered them animatedly while Ryan threw him a loving smile as if to say "Look at this brilliant kid we have." He hoped his returning smile conveyed the same adoration, but concealed the overwhelming hope.

They'd started tag-teaming Finn at bedtime, meaning the six-year-old had no chance; he usually conked out now by eight-thirty instead of the nine or nine-thirty that Angel could manage on his own. He hated that Ryan hadn't been around recently to help with the routine. Without him, they floundered. He didn't want his excitement at the prospect of Ryan being around more often to scare Ryan off.

They picked up the kitchen and living area and were ready to watch their favorite detective show when it came on at nine. Angel played with Ryan's fingers during the show; he liked watching Ryan flex them after Angel had contorted them in every which way. Ryan barely even glanced at his antics until Angel sucked a finger into his mouth.

"Babe," Ryan said, the last note going up in question. Angel smirked at him and immediately shifted to straddle his hips, pressing his erection into Ryan's groin.

"I want you to fuck me," Angel said.

Angel loved controlling Ryan like this. It was so easy to send him into the sex-daze; so easy to move the fingers he was just playing with to his ass and the other hand to inside his unbuttoned pants. Beneath him, Angel felt the stiffening weight of Ryan's dick, and he ground down against it, directing their movements, guiding the rhythm until Ryan moaned into their messy kiss.

When Ryan's arm slid around Angel's waist to lift him, it caught Angel off-guard. He hadn't seen Ryan's unbridled strength since before he left to fight overseas and now, apparently, it was back. Angel had forgotten how quickly Ryan could turn the tables and manhandle him wherever he wanted to. Part of Angel was a little disgruntled at having his plans disrupted, but his cock, leaking a string of pre-cum onto his belly, disagreed.

Ryan stumbled them into the master bedroom with Angel trying his best not to become any heavier in Ryan's arms. While Ryan did like to pretend he was all better, Angel saw the twinges of pain on his face every once in a while. Now, though, Ryan's mind seemed to be on anything but the pain in his leg. He slammed Angel effortlessly against the door, coaxing Angel's legs around his hips as he ground their cocks together.

"I want to ride you," Angel panted, his breath hitching in his chest.

"I don't know," Ryan hissed. "I think I like you just like this."

"Ryan," Angel whined, and a moment later, he was flung flat on the bed with Ryan right behind him.

"Get to it, then," Ryan said, shucking his clothes to the ground and throwing open the dresser for lube and condoms.

Ryan opened him roughly, his fingers deft and relentless, his eyes intent enough that Angel nearly came just from that. He liked the burn; it made his hips twitch back onto Ryan's fingers and his cock leak wildly. He went to straddle Ryan after barely three fingers, and Ryan made a noise of protest.

"I like it," Angel hissed into Ryan's ear, tugging on the lobe with his teeth. "I like when it hurts a little."

"Fuck, Angel," Ryan moaned. Angel felt Ryan's fingers dance from his hips, to his cock, to his thighs. Despite his words, the burn was almost too much, and when he was completely seated, he kissed Ryan to distract himself from the pain. Soon enough, he knew, it would shift into the luscious burn that set his every nerve alight, and when he felt it change, he threw his head back and moaned, letting his hips roll into it. Ryan was soon bucking underneath him, and Angel guided one of Ryan's hands to his needing cock. Ryan wrapped his fingers around Angel expertly and promptly began teasing the fuck out of him, swirling his thumb around the crown, but avoiding the slit, then skimming down to the base with just too little pressure, over and over until Angel was keening.

"I swear to God..." The sentence was cut off mid-breath as Angel felt himself seize up, pulsing between their bodies after Ryan nudged his prostate. Ryan smirked up at him and Angel kissed it off his face. Ryan flipped their positions, hitching Angel's thigh over his shoulder and pumping a few more times before collapsing onto Angel's back. When he gained back enough strength, Ryan flipped Angel over onto his back again. The move was enough to get the attention of Angel's dick, and five years younger, he'd have been ready for round two. Now, it just made his skin tingle pleasantly as Ryan licked the cum off Angel's stomach before pulling him flush against his warm body, their legs slotted together, and Ryan's face hooked over Angel's shoulder.

***

Ryan signed his studio lease for the first of April. Mike and Travis helped them pack up his apartment on base, and then helped again with unloading all of his stuff at Ryan's new place. He didn't have a lot of his own furniture, which surprised Angel. Ryan explained that he didn't have much because most of the base apartments were furnished, and he'd always been in the barracks. All he had was the stuff his mom had shipped from storage. The futon, he bought when he was at West Point, and the mattress was from his room at home.

They bought Mike and Travis craft beer and two pizzas for their efforts. Travis bitched about the strain he'd gotten in his hamstring, but seemed placated when Mike promised him a massage when they got home. They didn't ask Travis and Mike to stay to unpack the knick-knacks. It felt too personal. Ryan was almost worried to do it with Angel, but Angel made it easy. He didn't comment, just observed everything with careful eyes, as if he were trying to inventory it all in his mind. The knick-knacks were old, anyway; all the newer things had been left in boxes in different areas in Angel's apartment.

When they were done unpacking for the night, they fell asleep in a heap on the bed after an exchange of sloppy blowjobs. The next morning, they were both sore, and yet, instead of unpacking more, they made a mutual decision that christening every surface was a better use of their remaining strength. In the afternoon, there was a light rap on the door: Finn with Rosa in tow. Finn was grinning brightly at them.

"What are you doing?" he asked sunnily as he glanced around the room.

"Unpacking all of Ryan's boxes."

Finn's face actually dropped, and he lost his sunny disposition. He crossed his arms, kicked a box sharply, and ran out of the apartment.

Angel and Ryan shared a shocked look. Angel sprinted down the hallway after him, and Ryan could see Finn maniacally twisting on the handle to Angel's apartment. Angel let them both in, and Finn sprinted away from him again. Angel turned to Ryan and made a shrugging gesture before waving Ryan back into the new studio apartment to go on unpacking.

After a half an hour, Ryan got worried and locked up before heading down to Angel's— *their*— apartment. He slipped inside to find Angel sitting with his back against Finn's door, talking soothingly through the wood. Ryan raised an eyebrow and received a shrug in return, as if to say that Angel still didn't know what was wrong. Wordlessly, Ryan slumped down by the door, and Angel smiled, scooting over to make room.

"Buddy," Ryan started.

"Ryan?" Finn asked, sounding insanely hopeful.

"Yeah," Ryan reassured him. "Yeah, it's Ryan, buddy."

Finn threw open the door like a popgun, and Angel and Ryan nearly toppled backwards. Ryan felt tiny arms wrap around his neck from behind in a vice grip and he chuckled, pulling Finn off his back so he could look at him properly. Ryan wiped the tears from beneath Finn's eyes and shushed the little hiccups with soft sounds and a big hand on Finn's back.

"I thought you were coming to live with us," Finn wailed.

"Of course I am. I told you that," Ryan told him.

"Then why were you unpacking your boxes in that other apartment?"

"Well," Ryan began.

"It's complicated, kid," Angel cut in. "But Ryan is coming to live with us here full-time."

"Promise?" Finn asked.

"Promise," they said in unison.

He still looked unconvinced, so they showed him all the boxes Ryan had left all over the apartment. Finn was almost crazed as he ran to each box, throwing open the lids, and peering at the contents.

"Calm down, you don't want to break anything," Angel said gently.

"But I just want him to stay," Finn whined.

"I promise, I'm staying," Ryan said, picking up Finn and holding him close. "Whether or not the boxes are unpacked doesn't matter to me."

Chapter Fourteen

Angel was wrapping up his work in preparation for six days of vacation when his phone skittered across his desk with a text message. He glanced at it and picked it up with a smile, assuming it was a text from Ryan about dinner or packing for Myrtle Beach. Instead, it was a message from Rosa. Her boyfriend has gotten tickets to the Mets game from his dad, and she wanted to know if Finn could go. Her boyfriend was bringing his younger brother, and he was close to Finn's age. Angel sent back an affirmative text message and called Mrs. Hardy and Finn's school to let them know that Rosa would be picking him up.

At first, Angel didn't even consider what he and Ryan could do with an empty apartment other than pack for their trip without little hands taking more out of the suitcase than they put in. It hit him when he was driving home that they didn't have to be quiet tonight; they didn't have to wait until after ten, and his foot pushed down the accelerator a little more. He got home before Ryan and ordered a pizza that would be there in an hour and a half.

He was thinking of all the stuff they usually couldn't do, and already, he was ridiculously hard against the zipper of his chinos. If Ryan didn't hurry up, he'd have to take matters into his own hand—literally. He heard the key shift in the door, and he nearly skipped to see Ryan.

"Hey, babe," Ryan said, when he saw Angel walking toward him.

Ryan toed off his shoes, and Angel pushed him promptly against the front door. Ryan let out a surprised huff, looking at Angel questioningly, but Angel only threw him a dark look before ducking his head and mouthing at Ryan's neck, right over the spot that seemed to be hardwired to his dick. Ryan's hand found Angel's side and Angel bucked forward, trying to draw attention to the fact that his jeans were already half-unbuttoned.

"Where's Finn?" Ryan asked, when he regained his wits.

"Mets game with Rosa."

Ryan smiled and his hands immediately shifted to Angel's hips. His fingers moved to the band of Angel's boxer briefs and soon enough, they were wrapping around Angel. Angel allowed himself to sink into the sensation for a moment, the blessed relief, before he took a breath and pulled back, sinking to his knees, relishing the way Ryan's mouth fell open in appreciation.

He made quick work of the blowjob, tonguing at Ryan's crown until Ryan was moaning incoherently, fingers buried in Angel's hair. Angel swallowed rhythmically and pulled off with a shit-eating grin on his face.

"Jesus Christ, Angel," Ryan muttered, when he could finally talk.

"That's just the beginning, babe."

"Fuck," Ryan whispered. "Are you trying to kill me?"

"What a way to go."

186

"Not today, babes."

"Pizza will be here soon."

"Better return the favor quickly, then."

Angel eyed him under his lashes as Ryan dragged him to the couch and shoved him onto it. Ryan made short work of Angel's boxer briefs, palming him and mouthing at the slick tip of his cock until Angel was groaning, fisting a hand in Ryan's longer hair and guiding him to take him fully. Angel came quickly, Ryan getting better at this with every attempt, and Ryan wiped a smear of cum off the corner of his mouth before leaning up to kiss Angel again. When the buzzer trilled, Ryan tucked himself back into his pants and buzzed up the deliveryman. They ate quickly in relative silence, the air thick with a warm combination of satisfaction and expectation.

After they finished eating, Ryan grabbed the lube out of their room and opened Angel up, bent over the couch. Ryan fucked him right there, holding Angel down as he rocked his hips hard against Angel's ass. When Ryan finished, he flipped Angel over one-armed to suck him off again, two fingers working in and out of Angel's stretched hole, and Angel babbled obscenities as he came down Ryan's throat for the second time that night.

When they could move again, Ryan dragged Angel to the bedroom and into their bed. Angel made a protest about having to pack, and Ryan groaned and begged for just a few minutes of rest. In any event, they both fell asleep and didn't wake up until nearly ten.

Angel swore, throwing himself out of the bed in search of the checklist that he had made over two weeks ago. Ryan couldn't summon the energy to do more than start throwing t-shirts from his closet into a bag until Angel glared daggers at him. The soldier in him sat up at that, and Angel handed Ryan his own personal checklist for his bag. Ryan scoffed at the items until Angel reminded him how, when they went to stay at Travis and Mike's, he forgot socks, a toothbrush, and his pills; thankfully, Angel had seen the pills on the counter and thrown them into his bag.

By midnight, they'd finished packing and were watching some home improvement show that Ryan liked. Angel had fallen back into playing with Ryan's fingers again, kissing Ryan's random moles and freckles. Rosa knocked on the door almost on cue, and her boyfriend was holding a sleeping Finn. Ryan took him gently and carried him to his room.

The next morning, they left at ten to make sure they could check into their hotel in Richmond by four in the afternoon. Finn was still tired from his late night out with Rosa, so they ordered room service and a movie that wasn't even out on DVD yet. Finn fell asleep between them on their bed, and Angel transferred him to the other bed when they were ready to go to sleep.

They left early the next morning for Myrtle Beach. Everyone was up at the crack of dawn from their early night. They switched drivers every two hours, with the passenger reading the directions and manning the stereo. Finn was content in the backseat with his stack of books from the library, and the coloring books Ryan bought him that Angel had scoffed at.

Their hotel had a water park connected, and Finn begged them, with a yawn, to go to the park as soon as they were in their room. Angel wanted nothing more than to unpack and organize the room for the rest of the trip. He could feel the anxiety of having an unorganized room building up, as well as the dread of a confrontation on vacation. Finn sighed when he saw Angel start meticulously unpacking, and Angel was braced for the pouting and protesting when Ryan wrapped his arms around Angel's waist and hooked his chin over Angel's shoulder so his mouth puffed warm breath on Angel's neck.

"I'll take him down," Ryan whispered into Angel's ear. "Get him out of your hair, if you want?"

"Really?"

"Course," Ryan laughed, and Angel shivered when Ryan's lips unintentionally grazed over the sensitive spot below his ear.

"Can we? Please, Daddy," Finn said, grabbing his swim trunks out of the bag.

"I should say no just because you're nosy and eavesdropping."

Finn crossed his arms over his chest, and his eyes welled with tears. "But I won't, because you two will just make my life more difficult," Angel added.

Ryan snorted and Finn squealed as he sprinted to the bathroom to put on his swimsuit. Ryan rummaged through his bag to find his trunks, and

Angel sighed dramatically when Ryan left his bag haphazardly open.

"Angel, you need to relax; it's vacation," Ryan said, when Angel immediately started refolding Ryan's clothes.

"When I was little, I never packed enough," Angel said as he started transporting the clothes to the dresser under the TV. "But then, one time, I forgot Finn's special prescription formula when we flew to New York when he was an infant. His colic was so bad that night because we had to feed him regular formula."

"But he's okay and he will be okay. I think he'll be better if you come down with us, though."

Angel shrugged as he set the first aid kit next to the sink. Finn emerged and pushed Ryan toward the bathroom to change into his trunks. When he was done, Angel was barely finished with the small bag he brought. Ryan grabbed Angel's hand and pulled him to his chest. He kissed him softly. Angel didn't return the kiss and gently wriggled out of Ryan's embrace.

***

Finn immediately sprinted to the elevator and pressed the button. Ryan met him just as the doors were opening, and they climbed onto the elevator, following the signs to the water park.

When they walked in, Finn wasn't nearly as excited. There were a lot of people walking around, and the focal point was an intimidating slide. Finn slid his hand into Ryan's and pressed himself against Ryan's side.

"What do you want to do first, bud?"

"I don't know."

"How about we do the lazy river first?"

"Okay."

Ryan grabbed them a two-person inner-tube and held Finn's hand until he was climbing onto the flotation device. Ryan lay silently unless Finn spoke directly to him. After a little bit, Finn was excitedly pointing at things he wanted to do.

"Can we go on the slide?" Finn asked, as they tumbled out of the tube to climb up the stairs.

"If you want to," Ryan said.

The line was stupidly long, but Finn didn't seem to care as he rambled about everything he wanted to do. Ryan worried a little when the operator told Finn to not let go, but he didn't, and Finn got off the ride already giggling excitedly about wanting to go again. Ryan convinced him to wait for Angel for the next ride. They ended up at the kiddie pool, where Finn played under the different fountains as Ryan sat on the edge of the pool. Every once in a while, Finn would run over to talk to Ryan, but he seemed content to play in the water by himself.

"Your son's very cute," a woman said, as she moved to sit next to him.

"Thanks," Ryan said, barely glancing at her. Even still, he noticed she was attractive. It didn't take him long to figure out that she was definitely trying to flirt with him, and his suspicions were doubly confirmed when a possessive hand fell on the back of his neck.

"Hey, babe," Angel said, loudly enough for the woman to hear, and Ryan wanted to laugh at both Angel's possessive expression and the woman's look of surprise. Ryan gave him a quick kiss, but Finn had already noticed Angel and was running over to them, begging Angel to go on the big slide. Angel made up a flimsy excuse, but Ryan didn't want to call him out on it, so he took Finn again. Angel waited at the bottom of the slide for them.

They went back to their room to change, and then headed to the beach to find dinner. They fell asleep quickly that night, exhausted. The next morning they had breakfast in their room and then headed once more to the beach. Angel stayed yards away from the tide, which confused Ryan, because he was the one who suggested the beach vacation. When Ryan and Finn took off toward the ocean, Angel yelled at them to come back— "Finn, come here."

"No, you come here, Daddy," Finn yelled back.

"Finn Posadas, come here right now. You don't need to be in the water," Angel ordered.

Finn turned and stalked sulkily towards him, Ryan at his back. Ryan knew Finn was just as confused as he was. He wrapped their fingers together and started to drag Angel toward the ocean, but Angel dug his heels into the sand.

"What's wrong?" Ryan asked.

"Nothing, you were just too close to the water."

"That's kind of the point of a beach, babe."

"I can't swim," Angel mumbled.

"That's okay, I'll save you," Ryan said.

"You're ridiculous."

Ryan tugged Angel down toward the water so the tide licked at their ankles and calves. Finn played in the water further than Angel would've liked, but when a big wave came, Ryan scooped Finn up into his arms to keep the water from knocking him over. He didn't miss the reluctant smile that tugged at Angel's lips.

They had fun at the beach. The kind of fun Ryan never thought he'd get to have with a family of his own. They built sandcastles, played in the waves, ate ice cream— the works. An older woman told them how beautiful their family was, and Ryan couldn't stop grinning for the rest of the day. That night, when they returned to the hotel, Finn fell asleep right away. Angel curled up on Ryan's chest as he flicked through the channels.

"I love you," Angel said, tilting his face up to look at Ryan.

"I love you, too," Ryan responded, with a kiss to the forehead. "And I love Finn too."

Epilogue

"It's been a big three days, huh?" Angel said, wrapping his arms around Ryan's waist and kissing the back of his neck.

"Mmhm," Ryan hummed, moving the wooden spoon through the chicken stir-fry he was making for dinner. 'Big' was an understatement. The world felt like it had shifted on its axis, and the fact that Ryan was still there cooking stir-fry in their kitchen seemed absurd now. It seemed as if everything had rushed together at once: the end of Don't Ask, Don't Tell had been announced, and even before it could come into force, New York had legalized equal marriage. It was as if, all at once, the world had rectified everything that might have caused a problem for Ryan. He still couldn't quite believe it. Now, it was the end of September, 2011, and while at this time last week, Ryan wouldn't have been allowed to mention Angel at work, he was now free to keep a photo of him and Finn on his desk if he so chose.

"I was thinking that maybe we should plan something," Angel said.

"Like what?" Ryan asked, starting to turn into Angel's arms, but Angel let go gently, taking a deep breath.

Angel's heartbeat was deafening as he sank down onto one knee.

"What are you doing?" Ryan questioned.

"Ryan Garry," Angel said, too quickly, "will you marry me?"

"Jesus, Angel!" And here was the last ridiculously unexpected cherry on the cake. Ryan grasped at it before it could disappear. "Yes, yes, yes," he declared, pulling Angel to his feet.

"I had to do it now," Angel said into Ryan's mouth. "Otherwise, I thought I'd lose my nerve, and you would do it instead. So I got the ring today, and I had to do it. You don't have to wear the ring if you don't want to."

"This was perfect. And of course, I'll wear the ring."

"Your idea was probably more romantic."

"Angel, this was perfect," Ryan said, kissing Angel softly as he slid the ring onto Ryan's finger.

"No, it wasn't, but thanks for the sentiment."

"Is dinner ready?" Finn asked, cutting off Ryan's protest as he walked into the kitchen.

"Yeah, kid," Angel said.

"Finn, what do you think of me and your dad getting married?" Ryan asks.

"You are married," Finn said plainly. He grabbed a juice box out of the fridge. In the high chair by the table, Arya, the little girl they (or, officially, Angel) had adopted the previous year, was shaking her little fists. Finn grabbed Arya's sippy-cup and put it on her high chair. "You're our parents, you live in the same place, you take care of each other when you're sick, and you love each other. Isn't that what married people do?"

"Yeah, but before, we couldn't be married properly, because Papa would've been fired from his job, and it was illegal in New York," Angel explained.

"That's stupid," Finn commented, and his face scrunched.

"You're right," Ryan said, taking his habitual seat at the dining room table.

"Papa," Arya demanded, and Ryan looked over at her. She opened and closed her little hands and then smacked them on the tray. Ryan had chicken and vegetables ready, without spices and sauce, which he cut into tiny pieces for her.

"Hungry, baby girl?" Ryan asked, and Arya babbled happily at him.

"We got to let it cool," he told her.

She waited patiently for maybe half a minute before she implored again, "Papa?"

"Hold on," he said as he served himself and Finn.

She swiveled in her chair and looked at Angel as he loaded his plate up. "Dada?"

"You're an impatient one; Papa's making sure your tiny mouth doesn't burn."

Her face crumpled a little and she began to whimper; Ryan explained again, "It's too hot, petal."

"Ari, look at me," Finn said, crossing his hands over his eyes in a game of peekaboo. She sniffled the first three times, but the fourth time, she giggled. Finn continued to amuse his sister until Ryan was content that her food had cooled enough to set it on her tray. She immediately seized a piece of baby corn and gnawed on it, making little pleased noises as she munched on her food. They all began eating, and there wasn't any talking, which let Ryan know that the stir-fry was pretty good.

"Is that why you couldn't get me at the hospital when I broke my foot?" Finn asked suddenly.

"Yeah, that's why we had to wait for your dad to come before I could come see you."

"Will you be able to come get me if you guys get married?"

"Well, that's a different process," Angel interjected.

Finn nodded introspectively and clarified, "I want you to be able to come get me, Papa."

"Me too," Ryan assured him, and that seemed to resolve it for Finn. He went back to his meal, but Angel wouldn't look up at Ryan. He was worried, and he knew he shouldn't be, but he was. The rest of dinner, he could feel Ryan's puppy-dog gaze boring into him, but he kept his eyes on his plate and methodically speared each item.

Arya went to bed first. After a few board books, she easily flopped into her crib. She was asleep when Angel went to check on her fifteen minutes later. They turned off the TV at eight, and Finn knew that was his cue to go to his room. Finn got ready for bed, and they read a chapter of his current school book together.

Ryan was doing some work when Angel was done reading, so Angel sketched. He drew Ryan's hands as they moved across the keyboard, paying close attention to the new addition to Ryan's left hand. He felt elated, possessive. Every once in a while, Ryan would stop typing and twirl the ring around his finger as he read something, a little grin on his face. After sketching, Angel's fingers itched to paint and find the exact tone of Ryan's skin and the platinum band against it. Ryan had started to glance at him more, and he knew it was sometimes distracting for Ryan when Angel sketched him, so he set down the pen. Painting could happen later.

Ryan finished his work before the news came on at eleven. They headed to their room to watch the news and go to bed. Ryan immediately flopped onto his side, and Angel felt a vague wave of disgruntlement. He'd been expecting a bigger reaction from him— a blowjob at least, after today. Ryan never laid like this unless he was mad at Angel, and he'd seemed so happy about the ring. Angel couldn't quite place what he'd done. He slid his fingers into Ryan's hair and a minuscule tensing of Ryan's muscles made his stomach drop.

"I love you," Angel said softly.

"I love you too," Ryan responded, but he didn't move.

"I can't wait to marry you," Angel whispered, trying again.

"Me too."

Angel kept his hand on the back of Ryan's head, a gesture that would usually relax Ryan. Normally, he would quickly fall asleep, but Angel could tell he was purposefully evening out his breaths, which sounded forced and calculated.

"What's wrong?"

"I love Finn and Arya."

"I know."

"I want to adopt them."

Angel remained silent. Hope was swelling in his chest, mixed with disbelief. He should have expected this, but somehow, he couldn't bring himself to. He never expected much. Maybe that was his problem. Ryan was upset, he could tell.

"I want to be able to get them from the hospital if they get hurt. I don't want people to question my relationship to them. I want to be responsible for them. If something ever happens to you, I want them to stay with me."

"It's a lot of responsibility."

Ryan laughed. "You act like I haven't been doing it for over two years with you."

"But it'll be different."

"Yeah, I won't have to worry about seeing my kids if something happens to you or if something happens to us. I don't want to have to worry about the generosity of others. I want everything that comes with legal responsibility."

"I'd never keep them from you," Angel pointed out.

"That's not the point. I don't want my relationship with them to be contingent on my relationship with you. I want us to be equal when it comes to them."

Angel took a breath. "Are you sure?"

"More sure than I have ever been about anything. Even if we were not getting married, I'd want to do this, Angel. They mean everything to me."

"Okay," Angel said finally. "We'll start the process tomorrow."

"Thank you."

Ryan finally flipped over, his fingers seizing Angel by the hips, and Angel felt his stomach drop with a different kind of pleasure. If the blowjob that followed felt like the best he'd ever had, it might have had something to do with the sense of joy finally realized that was swelling all throughout his body, alongside whatever Ryan was doing to his cock.

It took over two months to finalize the adoption, but the day that it came was more exciting than Angel expected. They couldn't wait for the birth certificates to arrive, proof that they were Ryan's children too.

Nothing changed in any fundamental way. It wasn't as if Ryan wasn't acting as a parent before. This just legitimized their relationships. It also took an extraordinary burden off Angel's shoulders. Angel felt more comfortable now, as if maybe, however unconsciously, he had seen their relationship as conditional. Angel knew Ryan was adamant not to let Angel's hang-ups cause a rift in their relationship, especially when that was what Angel was expecting.

"Congratulations on becoming a father of two," Angel commented in bed that night with his chin on Ryan's shoulder.

"Thanks."

"I'm glad you're going to be my partner in this."

"Me too."

"I'm sorry if I ever made you feel like I didn't want you to do this."

"I get it," Ryan assured him, softly.

"But you shouldn't have to," Angel said. "Seeing how excited Finn was... it made me hate that I made you doubt whether or not you should do it. He already sees you as his dad, but others might not. It would only be a detriment to him if you hadn't adopted him. I feel like a fucking idiot."

"Don't worry about it," Ryan said as he pulled Angel closer to his body.

"I hate when you just accept the fact that I'm incredibly fucked up."

Ryan laughed and his eyes crinkled with it. Angel knew he was pouting, but it was just so annoying. Ryan kissed Angel's neck, and Angel could feel his resolve dropping. He wasn't angry; it was just exasperating sometimes to be with the most perfect man in the world. Ryan pressed their groins together, rocking his hips, and Angel made a mental amendment: The most perfect man in the world wouldn't be such a fucking tease.

"Ryan," he moaned, when he felt his dick hardening. He moved to shimmy out of his boxer-briefs.

"Let's get off like horny teenagers, instead of fathers," Ryan suggested, hooking a leg over Angel's hip. Angel could absolutely get on board with that. He curved his body against Ryan's and rocked up against him like a kid trying to get off before his parents get home, when really, their biggest concerns were Finn knocking on the door and Arya wailing from her crib.

His boxers were chaffing and dry-humping this way was always slightly unsatisfying in the end, but Ryan was making little noises like he didn't want him to stop, mouthing at the tattoo on Angel's left collarbone. His tongue followed the ridge of bone, teeth scraping after it in just the way that set Angel's skin alight with shivers. No teenager Angel was ever with was more worried about getting him off than him or herself, and Angel came first with Ryan's hand on the back of his neck and Ryan's mouth on his. Ryan thrust a few more times against him, but soon enough, he was coming too, panting breathily against Angel's neck. Nothing on earth was hotter than Ryan's sex noises, noises that could make Angel forget how uncomfortable it was once the cum started cooling in his boxers— but he couldn't forget about it for long. In the shower, he convinced Ryan into a follow-up performance, and this time, they made out slow and wet, a promise just as sincere and binding as the ring on Ryan's finger.

The next month was filled with wedding decisions that needed both of their opinions before Ryan went off to San Francisco for three weeks to work on an onsite project. Having such a short timeline had left them with few or undesirable or ostentatiously expensive options for most of the

202

things on their checklist. Ryan was frustratingly lackadaisical about each item and only had input on the food and guest list, which infuriated Angel for two reasons: One, he needed help, and two, he now knew how Alicia had felt, and he hated himself a little. Right before he left, Ryan got oddly interested in all the details, and Angel figured he was feeling guilty for his previous attitude. In retribution, Angel passed to him the task of finding entertainment for the reception. Of course, Ryan found someone easily, and Angel narrowed his eyes and critiqued the man's webpage for a good thirty minutes before accepting.

Their routine was thrown all out of whack when Ryan was gone, but they were getting a little more used to it, since this was the sixth time in the last two years that Ryan had to be gone for more than two weeks. Somebody in his family, or Ryan's, usually crashed at Ryan's studio and helped Angel with the kids, but they were never as in sync with him as Ryan. He'd always forget to tell them something vital, and one of the kids' schedules would be thrown off-kilter. This time, he forgot to tell Karen about Arya's physical therapy sessions, which Ryan usually took her to, and Finn was pissed when nobody picked him up early from Mrs. Hardy's on Wednesday.

They talked to Ryan every night after dinner, but the kids monopolized a lot of the talking time, and sometimes, Angel just wanted Ryan to himself. He knew that was selfish and they texted nearly constantly, but still, he didn't really like sharing— not even with his own children.

A week before Ryan was expected back, Angel got a phone call from him late at night. He'd been up painting, and it was nearly four in the morning, meaning it was one where Ryan was. His heartbeat accelerated because Ryan was not prone to calling him at ungodly hours unless it was an emergency. He braced himself for bad news and picked up the phone.

"Hello?"

"Angel," Ryan called into the phone. His name was slurred and dragged out on Ryan's lips.

"Yeah."

"I'm sorry, so, so sorry, babe," Ryan confessed into the phone, and Angel couldn't stop the metallic taste in his mouth, especially when Ryan wouldn't stop muttering the phrase under his breath.

"What are you sorry for?"

"The other workers wanted to take me out, said I deserved a proper bachelor party. I told them I didn't want to go, didn't need no stinking party. Loved you too much, basically already married, just wanted to go home. They said I couldn't go home, and so I should go out with them. Which seemed like... logical... at the time, but it was stupid. And I'm sorry."

A bubble of laughter burst over the phone to Ryan as Angel said, "Baby, that's nothing to be sorry for. I'm glad you had fun with your friends. Now, drink some water and take some vitamin B before you go to bed; otherwise, you'll definitely be feeling it in the morning."

"S'not that." And in his mind's eye, Angel could see Ryan drunkenly shaking his head as he heard Ryan's hair swish against the phone.

"Just tell me."

"Lap dance, they got me a lap dance and she was all on me. I might have gotten a little hard, but I was mostly just embarrassed. "

"Did you do anything about it?"

"No, I came back and called you. I miss you."

"Did you want her?"

"No, Angel, no, I only want you. I miss you."

"I miss you too. Don't worry, babe. I'm not mad."

"Are you sure?"

"Ryan, I've made more egregious errors that you've forgiven me for. I can forgive this one transgression."

A pause, and then Ryan's voice again: "I don't know what you just said, big words."

Angel couldn't help but laugh at that. "I forgive you."

"I love you."

"Love you too. Drink lots of water."

There was a faint giggle before the line went dead. Angel wasn't upset. He was a little jealous, but it was more because he wanted to be with Ryan. It was a harmless lap dance that somebody else paid for. He would've laughed if he was there, he realized. With that thought, any power that had to bother Angel was gone.

***

When Ryan returned to New York, there was still a number of little tasks they both needed to complete before the wedding at the end of November. Ryan could see the stress on Angel's face, but his usual tactics of slow blowjobs and sensual back rubs were not working. Angel was irritable; he snapped at Ryan, Finn and Arya. Finn nearly cried one night when Angel said he was too busy to read with him. Ryan curled up with Finn on his twin-sized bed and read a chapter, even though he hated reading aloud and stumbled over words. Ryan found Angel bent over his laptop at the dining room table, typing aggressively.

"What's wrong with you?" Ryan asked, frustration in his voice.

Angel laughed, the sound brittle. "There's so much to do."

"So, let me help."

"Everything is finalizing things I did while you were gone."

"I can figure it out."

"But it needs to be perfect."

Ryan sighed. "Angel, we're not perfect; our wedding doesn't need to be perfect."

"Yes, it does."

"Making me, Arya and Finn feel like shit isn't making our wedding perfect," Ryan accused.

"Go fuck yourself, Ryan."

"Well, you're definitely not going to, so…" Ryan trailed off as he walked away.

"It's like you don't even care."

"Wait, what? Excuse me, what did you say?"

"You don't care."

"About what? The wedding? Jesus, Angel, are you fucking kidding me? I care about our wedding, but I care about our relationship and our kids more."

Angel just made a face at him that was enough to say he was not kidding. Ryan closed his eyes for a moment, taking a deep breath. There was no reasoning with Angel when he was like that. Where words failed, action must suffice.

He strode directly into Angel's personal space, grabbed his face and kissed him. Angel made a surprised noise and their lips barely touched, their teeth clashing at first. Angel grappled with where to put his hands, but settled on Ryan's head, and in that moment, it was as if all awkwardness bled away and they were in sync again, the two of them. Ryan hitched Angel easily against the wall, encouraging the long legs around his hips; when Ryan lifted his cargo, Angel only groaned and tipped his head back, letting Ryan mouth his neck as they moved into the bedroom.

They fell onto the bed, the headboard knocking loudly against the wall, and Angel laughed whole-heartedly for the first time in days. Ryan smiled as he dug his face into the crook of Angel's neck. Angel roughly pushed down Ryan's pants and then got rid of his own. He pulled Ryan's sweatshirt over his head and placed open-mouthed kisses from his collarbone to his navel.

"Can I?" Angel asked, looking up at Ryan. His eyes were backlit, on fire. It sent a coil of equal parts anticipation and apprehension through Ryan. They didn't do this a lot, maybe a handful of times in the last year, but he nodded quickly. He loved the way Angel looked at him when he was inside of Ryan.

"Words, Ryan."

"Yeah, Angel, I want you to fuck me."

"Make love," Angel mumbled into his hip.

"Angel," Ryan hummed softly, and Angel kept nipping at his thighs and hips. "Angel, come here."

Angel snorted and moved until he was face to face with Ryan, then let himself be kissed, slow and steady. Angel reached for the lube in their bedside table. Angel knew well enough how Ryan liked a distraction, and he gave the kiss all he had, tonguing at Ryan's soft palate as he reached down with well-lubed fingers. Ryan gasped into his mouth, but didn't protest. After a few minutes, he added another finger and watched Ryan's face closely. There was a little sign of discomfort, but Ryan bore it manfully, pulling Angel to him harshly to nip at his lips. Once he was lubed, Angel pressed in slowly, opening Ryan up inch by inch, and Ryan closed his eyes, trying to breathe through the stretch of it in search of the pleasure he knew would come. Angel was moving so slowly, but the burn gave way eventually, until Angel's hips were flush against Ryan's ass. Angel trembled with the effort of holding still, and the pressure began building up a warm glow in Ryan's abdomen. The look of concentration on Angel's face made Ryan love him all the more.

"You can move," Ryan informed him softly. At first, Angel moved carefully, but after a few strokes, he began to pick up the pace, encouraged by the rocking motion of Ryan's hips and the way Ryan's back arched, his breath coming faster. Angel, unable to hold out, came first with a shout into Ryan's neck. He pulled out carefully, threw himself down next to Ryan on the bed, and wrapped his hand around Ryan's still-straining cock. Ryan bucked up into it immediately, already so close to the edge, and Angel tugged him over it easily, his breath warm on Ryan's neck.

"Chill about the wedding, okay babe?" Ryan murmured, his lids heavy.

"'Kay," Angel mumbled, and fell asleep.

He did chill, a little. Some things fell to the wayside, but nothing of utmost importance and nothing that was important to their relationships. Two weeks later, they were ready to get married.

The venue was beautiful and rustic, and Ryan couldn't think of a better place to get married. The setup was rather simple, just some elegant runners and a few bouquets. Nothing outlandish; that just wouldn't be them, much as that frustrated Travis. Mike ushered Ryan into his dressing room so he wouldn't see Angel. It was funny and a little endearing how people had been keeping them apart, when Ryan just wanted to see the slow smile and warm eyes. They hadn't willingly spent a night apart in over a year. Ryan had his pants and undershirt on when there was a knock at the door. He opened it to get bowled over by Finn.

"Papa," Arya chortled as she gestured to be picked up from the stroller Rosa was pushing her in.

"Hello, my beautiful flower girl," Ryan said, throwing her into the air.

"Papa," Finn lamented, tugging at his pant leg.

"Yes, bud?"

"It was weird without you today and yesterday."

"I was just gone for three weeks last month," Ryan laughed.

"But it was weird because I knew you were on the next floor, and I haven't talked to you all day. I usually get to talk to you when you go on trips for work."

"I missed you guys too."

Arya stuck her thumb in her mouth and pressed her face into Ryan's neck. She wasn't usually very cuddly, but Ryan was the exception to that rule. She loved tucking her face so that her nose was in the dip of his collarbone. He kissed her crown of curls and she sighed heavily.

"Tried to get her to take a nap; she wouldn't," Rosa informed him.

"Ari," Ryan admonished and she just dug her face further into him.

"Do you want me to take them with me?"

"Nah, we've got a lot of time before the wedding, and Angel refuses to give me anything to do."

"That's my brother for you."

210

"Go get ready. They can hang in here with me. Maybe I'll have Ari take a nap before she gets into her pretty little dress."

Finn immediately plopped down in the armchair in the dressing area and took out his tablet to play on. Arya looked at him, interested, but then brought her head back down on Ryan's shoulder. She shifted and whimpered a little bit.

"Come on, baby girl, you want to be awake for Daddy and Papa's wedding. You need to go to sleep now," Ryan cajoled. Ryan rocked back and forth, singing softly to her. Her eyes took a while to close, Ari clearly fighting it, but she did finally fall asleep, and Ryan sat down on the little loveseat with her on his chest. He leaned his head against the wall and fell asleep too. He woke up when the door opened and closed, to see Angel pressed against the door.

"Aren't I not supposed to see you?" Ryan asked groggily.

"Rosa told me she brought the kids, and you were going to try to get Ari to nap. I knew that meant you were going to be falling asleep too."

"We weren't supposed to see each other."

"Whatever," Angel laughed. "That's a straight wedding rule, right? Besides, I couldn't wait. I'm nervous as all..." He trailed off when Finn looked up sharply, anticipating the expletive— "And I missed you. You keep me calm, and I'm running around barking at people, and you made me promise not to ruin today. And I'm ruining it. And I wanted to make sure you were here. Rosa said you were here, but I just needed to see you. Make sure you didn't realize what a horrible mistake you were making."

"You're an idiot. Of course I'm here. You three are the best things that have ever happened to me. You're not ruining it; calm down and come here."

Angel slid into the small space that was left on the loveseat. Arya stirred, glanced at Angel, and reached one chubby hand out to put it on Angel's arm. Her eyes shuttered closed again.

"Anyways, I'm the one who probably would've slept through our wedding," Ryan confessed, and Angel laughed. "I didn't sleep well at all last night."

Angel leaned his head against Arya's on Ryan's shoulder and intertwined their fingers. Ryan kissed Angel's hand and closed his eyes again. They sat there like that until the door slammed open and Travis let out a frustrated yelp.

"You two lovebirds, up and at 'em, you need to get dressed and stop being all domesticated. You need to go back to your room. The little one is with the girls and the young gentleman is with Mike. You both need to get dressed in your respective outfits and stop breaking all the rules imaginable. You need a little separation before you say 'I do.' "

Ryan got dressed by himself, and there was a little part of him that was nervous, but it was his usual social anxiety. He was scared about looking stupid, about making Angel look stupid. He wasn't all that worried about the marriage itself. This ceremony was just a formality. He knew it was important to their moms and to the kids and to their friends, but he already felt married to Angel. He didn't need the government to tell him the status of their relationship, but it was nice that they could give this ceremony to the people they love.

Pete came in a half an hour before the ceremony. He looked good in his suit. He smiled, the usual wattage even brighter today.

"Nervous?"

"Only of looking stupid."

"Well, that's good. It's not like you two aren't basically married anyways."

"Yeah," Ryan agreed.

"I heard Angel is being a lunatic."

Ryan laughed and shook his head. "He wants it to be perfect."

"I wouldn't know whose wedding I was at if it were perfect."

"That's what I said."

"He thinks *you're* perfect, you know. That's why he wants to make it perfect."

Ryan scoffed, "He knows I'm not perfect. I can barely write a sentence without misspelling a word."

"But you're perfect to him."

"Pete, I hate when you do this."

"Do what?"

"Get all philosophical on me."

Pete laughed at that. "You're right, how 'bout I do a toast instead?"

"Booze, that's more like it."

Pete got them two craft beers that Travis demanded they have, and they toasted the wedding.

The cold, amber liquid felt good as it trickled down Ryan's throat. He chewed a piece of gum to get rid of the smell, and he enjoyed the slight looseness the beer added to his muscles. He didn't know if it was the alcohol itself or the mere act of drinking with Pete that gave him the boost of reassurance he so desperately needed.

Neither of them walked down the aisle. Instead, they opted to just meet each other at the altar, Travis by Angel's side, and Pete by Ryan's. Their kids, however, did walk down the aisle to them, Finn pushing Arya in a decked-out stroller. Finn stood pressed against Angel and Ryan held Arya. They said the traditional vows. Ryan had worried about not being able to articulate his feelings if they had to write their own. They involved the kids in the ceremony, offering them both necklaces to show their commitment as a family. Finn was elated and hugged them both tightly. Arya tried to pull hers off immediately to get a better look. When the officiant told them to, they kissed, and Ryan felt a spark in it that he looked forward to reigniting later.

It took the staff a little while to transform the space into their reception area, so they had a cocktail hour in the foyer area. Angel and Ryan took pictures with the kids, even venturing outside. The cutest pictures resulted from an accidental trip and the resulting cuddle session.

The reception was fun. Travis and Pete made long, boisterous best man speeches, constantly trying to outdo the other. Mike and Finn tore up the dance floor and made everybody laugh. Everybody was so happy that Ryan wanted the moment to last forever, although, of course, he knew it couldn't.

They dropped off droopy-eyed Finn and Arya with Rosa, who had already changed quickly into her pajamas. They headed to their room and Angel was kissing Ryan before they even closed the door. They were both nearly naked when Ryan's phone started ringing. Angel glared menacingly at him.

"I thought I turned that off, I swear."

Angel sighed, but rolled off of Ryan. "You might as well pick it up."

"Hello?" Ryan answered.

"We want to stay with you," Finn whined into the phone without greeting.

"But you're going to have fun with Aunt Rosa. She's going to take you guys out tomorrow."

"But we want to be with you guys. We just got married." Finn's statement made Ryan snort into his arm, but it also kind of melted his resolve.

"The kids want to come upstairs," Ryan told Angel, who vigorously shook his head no. "Finn says 'We just got married.' " Angel chuckled and Ryan could see him giving in.

"Okay, but you owe me," Angel said, and Ryan accepted that because Angel's threats usually worked out well for him.

They got into the sweatpants that they were hoping not to wear and waited for Rosa to bring the kids upstairs. There was a soft knock and then a lot of little knocks before they got to the door. Finn smiled up at them and ran to jump on the large king-sized bed.

"I'm sorry," Rosa said, but they shooed her back to her room, knowing it wasn't exactly her fault. Once the kids had decided they wanted something, they generally got it, come hell or high water. Besides, they were married now. There'd be plenty of nights for sex, plenty of wild showers and snatched moments and dirty weekends. But this day, for the four of them, this stood alone.

The four of them climbed onto the bed with the kids in the middle. The kids snuggled down quickly, and Arya's eyes were dancing closed before Angel even turned off the lights. Finn fell asleep quickly too, until Ryan and Angel were just staring at each other. They linked hands above the kids' heads and smiled at each other.

"I love you," Ryan said softly, and Angel smiled.

"I know."

There was nothing Ryan would have rather heard.

34775875R00121

Made in the USA
Middletown, DE
04 September 2016